Essex County Council

Many libraries in Essex have
facilities for exhibitions
and meetings —

enquire at your local library
for details

NIGHT AT THE CARN

Night at the Carn

and Other Stories

A. L. ROWSE

WILLIAM KIMBER · LONDON

This collection first published in 1984 by
WILLIAM KIMBER & CO. LIMITED
100 Jermyn Street, London, SW1Y 6EE

© A. L. Rowse, 1984
ISBN 0–7183–0511–6

Photoset by Scarborough Typesetting Services
and printed in Great Britain by
Biddles Limited, Guildford and Kings Lynn

Contents

		Page
	Preface	7
I	The Priest and the Pueblo	9
II	Under the Toyon Berries	19
III	The Persecuted Cleric	25
IV	Naboth's Vineyard	40
V	The Pinetum	47
VI	After Sixty Years	55
VII	His Reverence	62
VIII	The Room above the Cloisters	69
IX	The Paragon	76
X	The Conceited Scholar	88
XI	Mad Miss Moll	98
XII	St Carroc's Crucifix	108
XIII	Night at the Carn	118
XIV	The Beneficent Shoes	127
XV	The End of the Line	137
XVI	The Red Bicycle	147
XVII	The Lunatic of Landegey	155
XVIII	The Dream House	163
XIX	The Wax Doll	170
XX	A Holiday by the Sea	175
XXI	The Wise Old Serpent of King's Wood	180
XXII	Sailors' Orchard	186

For
Foy Quiller-Couch
in memory of
dear Q.

Preface

Historians are apt to be specially interested in the folklore, people and stories, of their native parish or county. And not only historians. When Hardy wrote his short stories, *A Group of Noble Dames*, they were mostly based on Hutchins' Parochial History of Dorset.

Similarly with Quiller-Couch, who knew Cornwall, Cornish folk and dialect to his fingertips. He was in fact not a historian, but a first-class short story teller, who wrote a number of classics in that genre — absurdly under-estimated and overlooked today, by people who have no idea of good writing, as he had and exemplified.

In a period of demotic social revolution the first thing that goes is quality, good standards — and of every kind, conduct as well as style: one has only to look round today. But there will always be a few, the elect, to set store by them and maintain them for themselves. Something of what I owe to Q. appears in my dedication, with undying appreciation, admiration and affection.

Acknowledgements are due, for a few of these stories which have appeared in *Blackwood*'s, going right back to Walter Scott — now alas, defunct, like many other good things in our squalid, insecure society; in the *Contemporary Review*, which goes back to the great Victorian days; and the *Yale Literary Magazine*, oldest literary periodical in the United States.

Trenarren, St Austell,   A.L.R.
Christmas, 1983

I

The Priest and the Pueblo

The Professor braked hard, and drew the car up on the very brink of the canyon. His English guest was alarmed, and inwardly angry. Good manners forbade that he should show it, especially to an American who had been so good as to bring him to this pueblo he so much wanted to see — the scene of such strange events, from another universe of experience.

All the same, he thought, suppose if the brakes hadn't acted in time! There they were on the lip of a direct drop of a mile or so.

What struck the visitor as he looked over the edge was the Silence. It was like something positive rising up to meet one — monumental, frightening. In its way more remarkable, because more strange — unprecedented in his experience — than the vast red, ochre and purple cliffs of all architectonic shapes, rising up on the opposite side and down the length of the canyon.

Recovering breath and temper, he looked down at the Indian settlement he had so much wanted to see: a group of adobe houses, and then what looked like cliff-dwellings in the side of the rock. Patches of bright green Indian corn beside the stream; a little yellow-clay church with bell turret at end, beside it a square, clean and smooth, of bare pavement taking the place of a churchyard.

The Professor was familiar with the place, and was well organised. Taking from the car an army knapsack that contained their picnic lunch, and a couple of stout knobkerries in case they met a rattlesnake, he led his guest a few hundred yards along the edge to where a crack in the cliff gave on to a track that made the descent.

The descent was stiff going, though the path wound and looped, zigzagged and returned upon itself so that the settlement at the bottom was mostly lost to view. Time enough to take in the vegetation, exotic to the English visitor fascinated by the difference of American botany and wild flowers, particularly here in the Spanish South-West.

They had come across semi-desert from Albuquerque, passing an occasional mesa, a mass of rock rising up like a cathedral or castle, mostly yellow clay-colour, with a flat plateau at the top. To the north, in that clear desert air, the Sangre de Cristo mountains, blood-red; but not the bright crimson of fresh blood, the darkish purple of dried blood, here and there still sifted with snow at the top.

Along the way, patches of grey sage-brush, dusted with the gold of Spring; and those familiar figures of the desert, joshua-trees, their fantastic gesticulating shapes like sign-posts or scarecrows − sometimes, thought the English visitor, given to imagining things, like men crucified, heads leaning over.

On the way down the yuccas were familiar enough.

'We call them Spanish bayonets,' said the Professor − apt enough for their sharp scimitar leaves. To the Spaniards they had been *candelas de Dios*. Clumps of manzanita clung to ledges wherever there was foothold for a shapely shrub with bare ruby trunk and stem.

Towards the bottom the presence of water was heralded by a change of vegetation: delicate feminine aspens with a shimmering fleece of gold, and then a clump of big cottonwoods, their spreading branches feathered with light fronds and twinkling leaves. A group of tamarisks reminded the visitor of his home on the coast of Cornwall.

No rattlesnakes. But, as they rested and ate their picnic

under the shade at the bottom, the Professor told his guest of a grisly experience he had had not so far away, returning to Albuquerque one evening.

Light was failing, and so was the car. Battery trouble? for the lights were dimming, the car slowing down. He thought of stopping, and getting out to investigate. Looking out, he thought better of it; for he found that the car was in the midst of an army of snakes crossing the road, coming down from higher ground to drink at the stream in an arroyo on the right.

Fortunately the car did not stop altogether, but at a snail's pace moved forward through the slithering mass. And then picked up pace. But it had been an eerie moment.

The Professor had been in the recent war. When in training in Texas, his group was to have taken an earth-wall at the run, and leaped it with full equipment. The first recruit took the leap with ease — and landed on the other side in a nest of rattlesnakes. That had been the end of him.

By the time the picnic was over, and they left the friendly shade for the sun-drenched pueblo, the sensitive visitor, a little on edge, was ready to expect anything.

But why was the settlement, to all appearances, deserted?

True, it was the siesta hour in Albuquerque — most people there would be taking their early afternoon rest, streets deserted.

To all appearances was the operative word; for the Professor knew, what his guest did not, that eyes, behind the slats of the window openings in the face of the cliff, were watching them. There were the ancient houses of the pueblo, box-like cubes one above the other, here and there a ladder to ascend. On the flat, a few more recent adobe houses nearer the church.

They approached the little chapel of the Santissima Trinidad, sanctus bell missing from the bell-cote above the entrance. Why? The door shut and locked. Why? The rectory, the priest's house, connected with the church by a roofed passage, also shut up. No one there. No one about.

They marched across the empty cemented pavement to look in through the windows.

'A parson could make himself quite comfortable here,' said the visitor.

Though the house was made of adobe and of one storey only, as usual, it was quite spacious: three rooms *en suite*, kitchen with big open fireplace, oven beside it, at one end; at the other, the roofed passage to the sacristy and into the church.

'Old Father Fogarty did,' said the Professor; and as they prowled round, he told his visitor the quite recent history of the place.

The rectory empty of furniture; the church too. Bare benches were there; but the altar was bereft of its usual furnishings: no candlesticks, no monstrance to hold the Sacrament; no images of the Saints or Mother of God in the usual tawdry tinsel and painted nimbuses that ornamented these Spanish-Indian churches.

The place was emptied of meaning, of the spirit that had dwelt within. Desolation all round. Looking in upon the scene, the sensitive visitor felt an intruder upon a secret — as indeed they were. The Professor, however, knew it.

Old Father Fogarty had made himself comfortable there for years. He had had a Mexican woman, from the village at the other end of the canyon — his parish — to cook and do other little things for him. He made himself happy on the pulque the Mexicans distilled for him out of the sap of their agave trees, and the Irish whiskey brought over across the arid wastes from Albuquerque.

An Irishman, he was at his ease with the primitivism of his parishioners, both Mexicans and Indians, and made no move to disturb their rites.

But a new Bishop was not pleased with the too cosy domestic arrangements of the rectory, and a parish priest sunk in sloth and drink. A reformer himself, the Bishop removed the old Irishman and put in an energetic young priest, who would clean things up.

Father Grossengut, as his name bespoke, was a German, and had rather less than the tact usual with his kind, and even more of their *Planmässigkeit*. He had a plan of campaign. He would begin with the Mexicans at the other end of his parish.

He was from North Germany: was he somewhat tinged by its dominant Protestantism? Or touched by the Jansenist spirit prevalent in the strict seminary in which he had trained?

At any rate, he was utterly unfitted for the goings-on of this remote world into which he had been thrown — precisely to reform them. He was scandalised, even appalled by the ways of his Mexicans in Holy Week — the Penitentes who, masked and half-naked, whipped themselves and each other in frenzy until their backs were bloody. Not content with that, they plunged cactus spines into their breasts and foreheads — to simulate the sufferings of our Lord under his Crown of Thorns. Steps led up to the Calvary outside the chapel there: the Penitentes had the habit of licking the steps to the Cross until the blood ran from their mouths.

Father Grossengut had some success in mitigating, though not altogether extinguishing, what he regarded as these horrors. He had the weapon of Confession he could use against his Mexicans — and, true to type, he had no hesitation in wielding it.

The Indians of the pueblo were a different matter. Though they came to Mass, they would not come to Confession. Somehow he could not reach them if he tried — and, without any intuitive sense, he did not try very hard. Even at Mass it gave him a slight unease to regard them in the mirror set at

13

the side of the altar, to keep a watch on any movement among them while his back was turned.

There was no doubt that, while they conformed externally to Catholicism, their real religion was a secret one of their own. Not so far from the canyon of Santissima Trinidad was their Holy Mountain, which no white man was supposed or encouraged to go up. In fact, the whites were actively discouraged, one way and another.

Within the Mountain were caverns, in one of them a sacred fire, never extinguished, which the Indians would visit at nightfall. In another was their god, a great snake, carefully tended: it was said that unwanted new-born babes were fed to it. An expeditious way of birth control, after all. And not so different from the ancient Greek − or modern Chinese − habit of exposing female infants on the mountain side.

Father Grossengut had little or no contact with the minds of the Indians of the pueblo, as remote from him as the caverns of their Holy Mountain − as to which he was insufficiently instructed.

What disturbed him, immediately under his own nose, eyes and ears, were the dances the Indians insisted on performing, at certain phases of the moon, in the graveyard immediately outside the church.

The Rector had not appreciated that the church had been built beside, if not upon, their sacred dancing place. When the Professor arrived at this point, his guest, something of an historian, recalled Pope Gregory the Great's advice in missionising the pagan Anglo-Saxons, to sanctify their holy places by building their churches on the spot.

'There they are − at it again,' the priest would say, aroused from sleep at midnight by the beating of a couple of drums, the soft pit-a-pat, pit-a-pat of many feet − like the pulsing of a disturbed heart. Then, at the end, an eerie cry like the howl of coyotes, baying at the moon.

Father Grossengut entered upon his plan of campaign — one, two, three: like Hitler with his fixed plan, first Austria, then Czecho-Slovakia, next Poland; finally Russia. And Nemesis. (The German priest might have been forewarned. But warnings, with them, are no use — a wall across the mind, reflected the traditionalist Englishman.)

The priest's first step was to get hold of the two drums. The headman of the pueblo came to protest. No use. The dances continued without them.

The earth of the graveyard had been flattened and pounded to the consistency of hard-baked mud by generations of naked dancing feet. Almost like cement — except that there was in it the life of earth, a certain give-and-take, like the palm of one's hand, the hard dark tan of an Indian's hand. (But what was being given, and what taken?)

Since the dances continued, without drums, still with that wild unnerving shriek at the end, the priest thought of another step in his campaign to end them. Church and churchyard lay open, hospitably, to the pueblo. He had a low wall built round from church-door to rectory kitchen, a semi-circle enclosing the dancing place.

There followed another visit from the headman. Did the Father not know that the people *must* dance their dance. Or else — what?

Father Grossengut had heard of the Hopi Snake Dance among the Navajos, not so far away — when the ritual dancers performed with live snakes in their mouths, bitten or not. And he had learned that the purpose of the dance was to bring up the spring corn, fertilise the earth — and it was followed by fertility rites, the sowing of the seed, human as well as vegetable.

The puritanical priest — no anthropologist — was not only contemptuous, but disgusted. Nothing of that kind of thing was to be allowed under his nose, eyes and ears at Santissima Trinidad.

15

The headman tried to explain.

'Dance not make corn grow', he said, dropping the definite article, as even the best Indian speakers of English did – giving the expression of their sentiments a curiously nobler, generalising sweep.

The priest learned that his Indians danced on the beaten earth of his churchyard to keep in touch with the spirits below, their ancestors. The coyote cry at the end was a summons to them for help.

This was no better in his eyes than a dance to make the corn grow – rather worse in his view.

The wall remained up. Not only that, but convenient bits of cactus, shards and broken glass were planted along it.

This was a provocation, which demanded a retort – and received it. One night, on retiring to his bedroom, which he had arranged comfortably with square feather quilt on top of his bed – nights were apt to be sharp – a rattlesnake was no less comfortably installed on the feather bolster.

This should have been a warning to him.

Not a bit of it. *Planmässig* as ever, he would go on to his final campaign and stop the dances for ever – and meet his Nemesis.

He had the bright idea of bringing over, all the way from Albuquerque, a couple of masons with a load of cement, to cement up the floor of the dancing place so that it could be danced on no more.

The pueblo took the message: no communication could get through between their naked dancing feet and the spirits below: no help from the earth.

The headman and the pueblo took counsel together. The decision that was arrived at was a democratic one, and unanimous.

On the night it was made, an unearthly silence prevailed in the community, and all the women were ordered to stay indoors.

In the pale light of a gibbous moon the menfolk drew around the sacred enclosure. A low wall was no barrier, and what to them a gash and a splash of blood?

The priest looked out and saw the silent shadows now within his wall, surrounding the rectory — sometimes a glint of an eye as they neared his window. What to do? There was no escape.

Father Grossengut was not without the courage of his race. He awaited his fate.

No coward, he took up a little crucifix from his prie-dieu and held it in his hand.

In the tense moments that followed he remembered what he had read of the great Indian Rising of two centuries before, when every Spaniard and priest was either murdered or harried out of the country. It was years before New Mexico was reconquered and missions replanted — many of them were not.

The shadows had no difficulty in infiltrating. What added to the horror was the silence. Not a word was spoken, by them or him, as he was bound hand and foot, and carried out to the dancing place.

Some thought entered his mind whether they intended to trample him underfoot and dance him to his grave.

But no — this was the twentieth century, after all. The pueblo had no mind to kill him, and risk punishment from the government. This was a religious affair. The priest was to be *carted* — carried ignominiously out of the community; such loss of dignity that he could never come back.

They might have taken him all the way into Albuquerque and deposited him on the steps of the Bishop's residence, to whom they owed Father Grossengut. But that would have alerted the city; more, it was contrary to the Indian sense of courtesy.

They left him, bound and tied as he was, on the roadside on the outskirts of the city, to be discovered and attended to by some good Samaritans early in the morning.

*

Of course, such an affront to Holy Church was indeed a religious matter. The Bishop had to reply in kind. The pueblo was excommunicated. No priest. No Mass. The very bell was taken away from the turret, so that no longer was its familiar call heard echoing down the canyon.

As the two visitors retreated from the scene of desolation, sadness over all, across the cemented dancing place, out through the gap in the wall, the historically minded Englishman reflected:

'Now, if this were the Middle Ages, instead of the enlightened twentieth century, the whole parish could have been laid under interdict — just like the reign of King John.'

II

Under the Toyon Berries

He was the son of a bishop – not that that did him much good, morally speaking. Not again that he was a bad man, rather a 'card', as they said in Edwardian days, when he was born. Anyway, the cleric had been only a colonial bishop, who died young, leaving his son, Mervyn, to make his own way in the world.

He made his way to Hollywood to become an unsuccessful script-writer, but did better for himself by marrying a rich widow of old Los Angeles family, as such families go. This enabled him to build up a collection of early Bibles and Prayer Books, the only tribute he ever paid to his episcopal background.

His wife was much attached to him, in spite of his vagaries and suspected infidelities. For he amused her, and had what it takes to amuse women: 'Never a dull moment,' she said of life with him.

For her part, she had her own resources, in both senses of the word. She was a horse-woman, devoted to her mount, and most days would go off riding up the canyons and foot-hills of the Los Angeles Mountains. And she had a fancy for animals, kennelling an opossum in her garden and putting out food for the shy little Californian foxes. She had a flood-light which caught them all feeding together at night from the trough on the lawn.

Perhaps Mervyn was part of her collection of only half-domesticated animals, for he always remained coltish and prancing. There was something irresistibly unadult and gay about him.

Financially, he was utterly dependent on her, with hardly any resources of his own, though he was up to some tricks. When Christmas came round she was in the habit of writing him a good round cheque, sometimes for $15,000, sometimes $20,000.

For weeks beforehand he would be on tenterhooks like a boy, wondering how much her present would be. She had a liking for music and, when the season came round, would take a box at the San Francisco Opera. Up they would go — he had no interest in music whatever; but he served the purpose of a very presentable escort.

He had a good presence and markedly gentlemanly manners; not particularly good-looking, but very masculine, which was what was required. He never looked the wrong way, so far as the sexes were concerned, as so many of the musical clientèle did. His leanings were very much the other way. 'A *gentleman* always props himself up on his elbows in bed with a woman,' he would say to the visiting Englishman, who found him an interesting study.

They had little in common, the English writer and he — except books and a certain modicum of snobbery. For, though Mervyn was now an American citizen, his father had been English, and Anglophily made a bit of a bond.

Mervyn sought to exploit it, and his new acquaintance watched his moves with amusement.

As part of the gentlemanly façade — or accepted status — Mervyn employed himself in various good causes. He wouldn't take a job, nothing so low as earning his living. He was Secretary — 'honorary' of course — of the local Technical College; this gave him the opportunity of meeting visiting celebrities, making himself useful to them — and touching them for his good causes.

His wife's well-known family was afflicted with alcoholism.

Both her brothers were affected. One of them, handsome as Apollo when young and a remarkable athlete, had been the apple of his father's eye; rich and utterly spoiled, a 'good sort' always ready for a drink, now a permanent wreck in a hospital, the fool. The other, temporarily rehabilitated, had a job as attendant in a local hotel — all he was fit for.

Nothing of this in Mervyn to worry Gabriella. On the contrary, he started an association for the treatment and rehabilitation of alcoholics, of which he made himself both secretary and treasurer. All was so gentlemanly and informal, he did not have to render account of any moneys received. What became of it? Or what came of it? Something was done for alcoholics, no doubt — perhaps especially for those in the family.

Nevertheless Ellice, the Englishman, was a little surprised when, quite early in their acquaintance, Mervyn presented the case of his alcoholics and suggested a subscription. Ellice, a teetotaller, declared himself far from sympathetic to the cause and expressed contempt for the fools who killed themselves with drink.

No opening that way — he had a rather suspicious mind, and less than no sympathy for what he regarded as weakness of character.

In return for small acts of kindness, motoring Ellice occasionally to a lecture engagement or a meeting, it became a regular habit with Mervyn to take a weekly lunch off Ellice. A successful writer, he was prosperous; but he noticed that Mervyn always made an exceptionally good lunch for the middle of the day.

Mervyn was Secretary — 'honorary' or not? — of an exclusive country club out in the foothills. This had its perquisites, among others enabling Mervyn to invite a guest for a free meal. Mervyn did not take undue advantage of this freedom. Only once did he invite his English friend to this paradise of green grass and trees amid the parched brown hills — the whole place liberally and expensively watered from the Colorado every day.

Ellice expressed no interest in membership, but Mervyn volunteered:

'I could get you made a member for $5,000 down.'

Ellice concealed his surprise − he had not expected this overture.

'But − some of the exclusive clubs in downtown Los Angeles expect an entrance fee of $25,000.'

Ellice thought this ludicrous, for company he did not wish for.

'Very well − $3,500 then.'

Ellice's suspicions were strengthened.

*

A side of Mervyn's life with which he was not acquainted, and would have had even less sympathy had he known, was Mervyn's relations with his secretary. For, with all his various activities − especially that at the Technical College − he needed a secretary. And in fact he led a double life with her.

How much of this was known to his wife? No doubt she had her suspicions, but Gabriella was a singularly detached woman, with her own interests, her horse (to which she was devoted) and her little menagerie in the garden.

Ellice would not have been surprised at this, for he soon realised that a certain disingenuousness was of the essence of Mervyn's character.

Mervyn found his secretary more rewarding − physically − than his wife. She had a voluptuous, rather serpentine figure, full lips and a way of waggling her hips that much appealed to his masculinity.

What did not appeal to him was her cultural pretensions. Not a concert in their vicinity but she made a figure in it, tall, heavy-lidded, suggestive eyes, winding her way sinuously to her seat. Her reading too − with little discrimination or judgment, she would a highbrow be, and wanted to be taken seriously.

They were much together over the business of the College. Gabriella didn't mind. Bent on leading her own life — with her bedroom upstairs, while Mervyn was relegated to the basement, where he had his bed and book collection both — she took no interest in his various public activities. She needed him only as escort — and, for the rest, few of her acquaintance, for all their money, had so agreeable, so un-demanding a husband.

The affair between Mervyn and his secretary continued satisfactorily for two or three years, when Gabriella fell ill. The secretary hoped for the best, and extracted some sort of understanding from Mervyn that he would marry her.

But his wife recovered. There was no possibility of Mervyn freeing himself — nor indeed had he any intention of doing so, giving up comfortable home with all found, the eager expectation of $15,000, $20,000, or even $25,000 at the end of a good year. Nor would he have dreamed of a divorce, and taking an ungentlemanly job for what? — a relationship that was beginning to pall, and might incur liabilities.

It might indeed — as was unfortunately, even dramatically, soon seen.

Recriminations followed between boss and secretary, as usual in such cases. The girl withdrew her 'favours', to her own disappointment as much as Mervyn's. He saw no reason for such fuss — he disliked the fuss women made anyway. His wife made none. A surge, if that is the word, of fondness for her took the place of more voluptuous pleasures with the secretary.

From this quarter a threat of blackmail followed — as also is frequent in such cases. No notice was taken, and then it was acted upon.

One fine spring day the secretary took leave of her job and spent the weekend typing letters to all Mervyn and Gabriella's acquaintance among the official and the best people in Los Angeles, telling the tale of her relations with her boss.

She then went down the drive and shot herself, spilling her blood beneath the blood-red toyon berries.

The scandal was great, and left its stain upon Mervyn's name. It ripped open the envelope of disingenuousness with which he had covered his activities.

It was then that Gabriella showed the stuff she was made of. She stood by him through thick and thin: 'Never a dull moment,' she parried with friends and critics alike. Whatever he may have done for the rehabilitation of her younger alcoholic brother, she now returned by seeing to her husband's social rehabilitation.

After a long holiday down the coast with her at Acapulco, he returned, somewhat chastened, to his good causes. And with a degree more candour, and less disingenuousness, than formerly. He one day went so far as to come clean with an acquaintance who suggested a return to script-writing, with the tale of his own life:

'Yes,' he said reflectively, 'there has been a good deal of tail in my life.'

III

The Persecuted Cleric

He would have been quite recognisable in the Zoo for an anthropoid ape, or not full-grown gorilla; for he was rather squat, broad-shouldered and long-armed, swarthy, bald yet very hairy, and he walked with the stealthy, sloping action of an animal. The one distinguishing difference was that he wore spectacles: without them he was as blind as a bat.

He combined the office of being Dean of Chapel in that ancient easterly institution towering over the inclement Fens, with being Steward, having to look after the domestic wants and feeding of the students. The first job was something of a sinecure, for few were those who went to chapel; the second was anything but a sinecure.

Both posts gave him equal anxiety, to which he was a willing prey: *Angst* was the element in which he lived and moved and had his being — the concept might have been invented to describe his condition, so well did it fit his every move, his cat-like awareness and stealth.

The Chapel in his care was the glory of the place, with its fan-vaulting and stained glass: it whispered the last enchantments of the Middle Ages to him in vain, for he was no aesthete and in theology a Modernist. He was so Modernist as to have very little belief at all; at one time he was in danger of losing entirely what little faith he had. Since he came of distinguished clerical stock and was suited for no kind of career other than the Church, this had brought him very near to a nervous breakdown.

Since then he had partially recovered his precarious

balance, but his shaky hold on faith made him all the more vulnerable a target for the militant Rationalists who were the most prominent members of that institution in the public eye.

One of them — the kindest, or the least unkind, at any rate, the most gentlemanly — was a famous mathematician. Two were professors of the dismal science, militant economists as well as Rationalists — at least members of the Rationalist Association, they were not so rational as they fancied themselves to be. Another was a zoologist, bearing a famous name, one of the family. A fifth was a classical archaeologist, rude and brash — he was found to be a millennium or so out in his archaeology of Macedonia. That did not make him any the less certain of himself; he led the hue and cry when the hunt was up for the poor Chaplain — who, as ill luck would have it, had the absurd name of Handsombody.

An element of irony in the situation was that he had been their candidate for the post of Dean of Chapel. After the 1914–1918 war, when these fellows returned from the front in Whitehall, they had been against having any chaplain at all. Imagine that splendid fane, with

> the high embowèd roof,
> With antick pillars massy proof,
> And storied windows richly dight,
> Casting a dim religious light —

imagine that famous building without chaplain or chapel services! (Well, one can imagine it half a century later, when egalitarianism — the logical consequence of their 'progressive' ideas — has ruined their Hall.)

The appointment of a Dean of Chapel prevailed only by the casting vote of the old Provost. So those enlightened spirits then concentrated on getting a Dean who believed as little as possible. The result was the Modernist Handsombody.

This placed him at their mercy — and they baited him unmercifully in Hall and Senior Combination Room. Already by nature a good deal of a masochist, he was tortured by it. He suffered silently, though trying to make an intellectual defence for himself — call it rearguard action or, more appropriately, redoubt — by throwing overboard everything that seemed unreasonable from the Rationalist point of view.

The result was that hardly anything of the Christian faith was left. It was not worth doing, for nothing would have satisfied them anyway. Appeasement never paying, it merely added to his sense of insecurity.

His life was already disconsolate enough on this side — were there any consolations to be found on the domestic side of his activities, from his contacts with his juniors?

*

He made up for inner insecurity by adherence to outward forms: he was a stickler for conventional routine, as a framework of support.

A young professor who was a regular professing Anglican became a member of that progressive institution. One day he went to Chapel on a weekday evening. None of the other professors ever did that. Was he welcomed by the Chaplain? Not a bit of it. On the other hand, the young man was a baronet in his own right, of a famous family. So what he got was the scrupulously phrased reproach, in the mournful tones of that funereal voice:

'I don't suppose you like to be told these things — but you should have worn a surplice.'

A little later the newcomer gave an address in Chapel, in which he mentioned the sacraments and divine grace — nothing out of the way, regular traditional beliefs. No felicitations from the Chaplain: coming away together, he said,

'You were *exceedingly* bold. You mentioned God.'

27

It was a pathetic little joke, but it showed that the iron had entered into his soul.

His own addresses — he would not call them sermons — were always essays in ethics, in which he did occasionally mention God. A scrupulous moralist, indeed an authority, when he was asked to give a series of lectures on the Gospels, he reached the conclusion that 'though we can make no certain contact with the person of our Lord in those uncertain records, and though we are vouchsafed no full sight of Him, it is yet the shadow of the hem of His garment that falls upon us as He passes by. Perhaps we must wait until we are ourselves beyond the veil, beyond this vale of tears, that the mystery may be revealed.'

That was as far as he could get in the recovery of his faith, which enabled him to hold on to the slippery slope of his post.

*

Were his secular activities any happier?

Well, he had a few intimates among the students, which gave him a kind of agonised happiness — they always *know*, recognise such things for what they are.

A former 'wet-bob' at Eton in paradisal early days, his foible was for rowing blues, upstanding muscular toughs. To one of them one day, with a hand on the well-developed biceps (he never explored further — unlike the celebrated economist, and the no less celebrated novelist, among the Militant Rationalists), he moaned:

'You must be *exceedingly* strong.'

'Exceedingly' was a favourite word with him: it told its own tale.

Another clue was his obsession against Noise — rather difficult to defend himself against, in an institution full of students. Here his defence-mechanism was to set a public example, and as Steward, in charge of their creature comforts, he was not without some constraint which he could exert upon them. But he preferred moral example, and precepts expressed with the odd accentuation of unexpected words, which sounded like a caricature of the Bloomsbury lingo of those Militants. To one student on his staircase:

'I have tried so hard to become *A* mouse.'

Himself padded around in rubber-soled shoes, or, in his own rooms, pussy-footed in carpet slippers.

To the young professor in the rooms beneath him:

'I would take it as a great favour if you would tell me if you hear *A* sound.'

After that, the newcomer hardly dared move in his room.

The Chaplain had a small obsession about mice — a Freudian symptom: a feminine characteristic. When a student came to him as Steward to complain of a mouse in his room, he was in his element: he of course had a mouse-trap. He lent it to the student for a week. After the week had elapsed the mouse-trap had not been returned. So the casual young man received a visit, with a scrupulously phrased reproach:

'What has become of *thee* mouse-trap?'

(He really believed that it had been lost — and one must never lose anything.)

'I lent you *thee* mouse-trap for *A* week. And now nine days have elapsed — and *thee* mouse-trap has not been returned. I shall be glad of its return,' etc. — a regular lecture followed on the ethics of borrowing and the obligation to return.

He was not without a sense of humour, but it expressed itself in such odd phrases that its subtleties were usually lost upon the ordinary man, normally imperceptive.

Passing a handsome freshman on his staircase one day, the Chaplain said, with a burst of geniality, but in that melancholy voice:

'I hope you will come in one day to tea with me.'

He did not specify a day, and the freshman didn't like to

intrude. Weeks later the youth had not turned up; passing him in the court, Handsombody said,

'Tell me, why are you *crucifying* me?'

What an inner world the tell-tale word revealed!

*

But would one have suspected that there was a vein of poetry, a certain sensuousness, behind this lugubrious exterior, always clad in clerical black, rubber-soled shoes or, in wet weather, goloshes?

As Steward he had chosen for himself the best set of rooms, at the top of a staircase, overlooking the Garden Court. Beneath was a border of roses, and his large fleshy nose, with its suggestive wobble, was very sensitive to scents. On hot, frustrated summer nights, he would linger over the border, occasionally emitting in school-girl language (another of his jokes):

'Thee *nif*! Thee *nif*!'

A giant wistaria clambered up the walls, embracing his windows in its arms, on its way up to the battlements it decorated with vine-like clusters of flowers. There on the leads he had constructed a pretty little arbour, shaded by the wistaria and flowers, where he drank tea. And also — for he was careful of his health — where he sunbathed in summer: his sanctum — perhaps there he felt safe.

Every eventuality was provided for. Each morning he awoke at six, in his chaste narrow bed, a picture of a handsome young Renaissance cardinal on the wall opposite. Having made himself a cup of tea, he worked in bed until his man-servant came at, precisely, half-past seven. He always left overnight a list of numbered things for his man to see to — so at 7.30 he put the man through his catechism methodically:

'Have you done No. 1, then No. 2, 3, 4?' in order.

It must be added that he made a competent Steward; nothing was neglected or overlooked.

*

Yet another way in which his aesthetic sense came out — or, as Freud would say, his repressed sensualism — was his collecting impulse. Collecting is well known to be an outlet for repression, and he was known to possess two collections.

One was a fine collection of silver, most of it kept in the bank. For he went in for rare Commonwealth silver, in which the institution was short. It had the finest collection of medieval silver left over from the depredations of the Civil War. But it had none from the Commonwealth and Cromwellian period; so it was generally hoped, as time went on and Handsombody aged, that his collection would come to the institution and fill the gap. That may have been his intention, before things took an unwelcome turn.

He had also had two or three Paul Sandby *gouaches* — not of the usual topographical water-colours. A connoisseur in his way, Handsombody responded to the few fully romantic landscapes of Sandby — to one in particular, of a splendid storm-scene, Gainsborough-like tree dramatically swaying, a figure crouched on steps in the foreground, in the background a shrouded castle as if it were that of 'Childe Roland to the Dark Tower came'. Of this, his favourite picture in his collection, Handsombody thrilled:

'It *burns!*'

*

The exercise of power is, naturally, another outlet for sexual repression. Handsombody had his sphere of power as domestic Steward, if not precisely as Chaplain too. But there was one more powerful than himself — the Vice-Provost, who ruled under an ailing and effete Provost. When the Provost retired, things would take a critical turn for Handsombody, for he had already taken up his stance against Haydon, the Vice-Provost, who was very likely to succeed.

How was it that Handsombody had come to turn against this popular and agreeable man, who had originally been one of his own supporters against the Militants? They had mostly moved away, the circle broken up with the years; as their persecution of him ceased it seemed almost as if Handsombody needed to elicit persecution, attract it to himself.

The Vice-Provost was not a man to persecute anybody, but he had a knack of getting his own way: he was persistent, and he never gave up. Handsombody on his former friend:

'He is a tyrant, with *A* will. You can feel it — like *iron* holding steady.'

So the Vice-Provost, with no hostile intent, was made the Enemy, in the Chaplain's fantasy, with its touch of masochism.

The Vice-Provost was a man of taste — only where Handsombody's was patchy, almost a foible, his opposite number's was all-pervading. Where there was an element of romanticism in the Chaplain, Haydon was all in favour of classical restraint. He had the great wistaria in the Garden Court trimmed, so that it did not grow out over the battlements in fantastic fashion. This wounded the Chaplain's fantasy, as it also denuded his sun-bathing arbour.

The Vice-Provost had merely meant to top and lop the wistaria so that it should not smother the architectural line. Handsombody's pronouncement upon this was:

'When Art comes into conflict with thee College, Art *always* wins.'

And from that time the Vice-Provost was framed as 'that bad man'.

He was in fact a good man, and the institution's interests always came foremost in his mind. Nor did he mean to offend Handsombody, for he hoped that the collection of rare silver, not to mention the pictures, would come to the institution in time.

*

As the election to the Provostship approached, the Chaplain came out in open opposition:

'*That* man — he is gaining more power *every* day that passes.'

To the young professor, now an elector:

'You do not know him. You will repent it. He will *tyran*nise over you.'

It was as if he courted defeat, for the election of the Vice-Provost was virtually certain.

At the election meeting he rose — superfluously inviting defeat — to say:

'I suppose that this time we do not have *thee* choir.'

The choir was famous — and it was the custom for it to sing from the gallery in Hall on the induction of a new Provost.

Of course they had the choir.

At high table on the dais there was a big Gothic chair for the Provost when he happened to dine in Hall. The Chaplain put forward the view that, since Provosts were technically guests of the Senior Combination Room, the chair could only properly be used by the new Vice-Provost as its head. On the first night Haydon dined in Hall as Provost, Handsombody marched up and — before anybody noticed — sat himself down in it, keeping the Provost out.

Over this there was a great dispute. It was at the time of the Fall of Singapore, and the sinking of the *Prince of Wales* and the *Repulse* — but a sub-committee was set up to investigate who had the right to sit in this chair.

There were two points of view — the Senior Combination Room point of view held that the Vice-Provost was its head, not the Provost, who was its guest. This was undoubtedly so. On the other hand, this was Hall. The view of the oldest member of the institution was requested: he replied that he was a hundred-and-four, and couldn't exactly remember. Precedents were then consulted, and it was found that the three previous Provosts had all occupied that chair.

Once more Handsombody had brought down Defeat upon his head — as if he sought it.

After that, whenever the new Provost dined in Hall Handsombody took his name off from dining, so as not to sit beside him. When the Provost appeared in the Court, Handsombody would turn back, so as not to have to pass or recognise him.

An awkward issue was now looming up. Handsombody was due to retire as Steward, but there was no retiring age for the Chaplaincy. Would he choose to stay on as Chaplain? If so, he would not be able to occupy his beloved set of rooms which he occupied as Steward.

While this critical issue hung over it, and no one knew the way it would go, an art-historian from the Museum, apprised of events, made an appointment with Handsombody to call one morning to see his Paul Sandbys.

He took along with him a companion on leave from the war. They had no idea of the revelation that awaited them.

*

November sunshine streamed in through all the windows of this double set which, they noticed, the old bachelor had annexed to himself. The occupant came forward from the interior of his bedroom, as it might be a ranging animal from the interior of its cage: bald but hairy, squat but with long arms, a bent anthropoid in black, a clerical monkey.

He briefly welcomed them with an understanding smile, half-smirk, then departed soundlessly for a lecture, leaving them at liberty in those rooms. They had a whole hour before them to take it in.

The occupant evidently recognised his affinities. From the electric light bowl in the ceiling dangled a chain of little apes, hanging each to each by elongated arms: a pendant horror. On the top of a bureau a woolly monkey peered down upon the alien intruders: like a cat he watched them, eyes fixed, unmoving.

Where other dons, arrested in adolescence, collected ducks,

owls, cockerels, tortoises, this one collected monkeys. There they were, a score of them, of all sizes and descriptions, big and small, arranged along the mantelpiece, on the tables, perched on ledges, waiting and watching to see what the intruders would do.

The quietness was unnerving; they could do nothing for minutes, they had so much the sensation of being watched.

Would the things themselves tell? indicate to their owner what they would do, or say, or *touch*? The sense of the life lived here was so powerful, so strong upon them, that neither could look at the pictures they had come to see. They felt themselves arrested. They drew a breath or two before, mesmerised, they began to look round − stealthily, as if they too moved on rubber-soles or in goloshes.

The *clou* of the sitting room was the writing table, with rug neatly folded over the chair where the occupant wrote, a footmuff for slippered feet below. For this was war-time: no fire permitted by this scrupulous conscience. But *every* eventuality was provided for: every contraption one could possibly want, blotter, paper-knives, paper-weights, ruler, semi-circular hand-blotter; an inverted bell full of pens and pencils, penknife, pen-wiper, multiple corkscrew-*cum* skewer-*cum* prizer-open of anything. *Two* reading desks in different places to catch the changing light, a rug at each, meticulous notes arranged ready for use.

Security above all things − nothing left to Chance, which was evidently regarded as malign, hostile.

What emerged was an aroma of Insecurity, the sense of a tortured conscience − anxiety − Guilt.

Among the snapshots, the photographs of the favoured few − brawny rowing men with muffled scarfs around muscular necks − were letters from them away at the war. Vistas opened up of affection, frustration, torment ('Why are you *crucifying* me?') − conscientiously turned into sponsorship, foster-parenthood − marrying them, christening their children. One of them was shortly coming to visit the Chaplain; newly married, his wife would be stopping with relations. (He was coming: she would not be wanted.)

The bedroom was a schoolboy's, spare, but not bare. From the bed one saw the Medici print of the handsome young cardinal, auburn hair, full sensuous lips, unrepressed. A complicated apparatus for shaving held a prominent place. Piled high above the wardrobe a whole stack of rugs; on the floor a dozen pairs of clerical shoes, several of goloshes, all black.

Adjoining was a little bookroom, shelved on every side and up to the ceiling — *two* ladders to get up to the top books. Nothing neglected, the mesmerised visitors observed: every cranny and orifice stuffed, bulging with papers, portfolios of correspondence, letter-files marked from A to Z, crammed.

'Like Parker's bookshop,' said the young companion. (But that was the old Parker's bookshop which William Morris had known.)

One tell-tale object hung on precariously from the corner of a shelf: a round and featureless hat of a Chinese mandarin, black with scarlet silk interior. The historian was reminded of the give-away of the scarlet clocks on the black socks of the Baron de Charlus.

Everywhere the dominant colour was Black, clerical black, with an occasional splash of scarlet within.

'Though your sins be as scarlet, yet shall they be as white as snow.'

*

They crossed to the second set occupied by the provident bachelor. A ripe and pleasant odour pervaded the dining room: Apples, Cox's Orange Pippins: rows of them high up on the top of everything, out of reach. On that level also, strung along cupboards and bureau bookcase, rows of pots of homemade jam, preserves, pickles. In the corner boxes and boxes piled up, containing cereals of every kind, Ry-vita, corn-flakes, Rice Crispies. Under pretty china covers on the dresser, cheese and his butter ration.

The young companion suddenly suggested the idea:

'He is keeping shop.'

Carefully placed beside each window — nothing over-looked, simply *nothing* wanting — was a long-handled window-opener with metal end. Those would be poles for putting up the striped awnings over the shop-windows, said the young soldier. The stores, the provisions were all around.

'That is not it, that is not it at all,' registered the historian, something of a poet, quoting Eliot to himself. Then what was it? What was the idea?

In the dining room were two or three more kettles — there had already been two in the bedroom, besides two in the bathroom. Why all those kettles? The little adjoining room here was full of stores — great boxes of tinned meats, potted paste, canned soups, extracts, fruits; tins and tins of biscuits — enough to stand a siege.

That was it! The dominant idea was that of a Siege. Here was the siege-mentality on every hand: the Persecuted Cleric of after the First German war had become the Besieged Man of the Second war.

That was it: he was under siege. Even the books revealed it. Why otherwise should he have *six* copies of Trevelyan's *Social History*, and not his subject? It must be because at the time the book was unobtainable.

Coming out again there was this sensation of everything on the *qui vive*, so very much alive, awaiting the return of the owner. How would they give him the *Word*?

The atmosphere was tense in the cold sunlit silence. November sun upon medieval roofs, Garden Court, and battlements. Yes — stacked in the corner of the stairs were the deck-chairs awaiting their turn to be needed, ready to be taken up on to the leads to the arbour for summer sun-bathing.

*

Night at the Carn

The young man found a phrase to describe it all: *La Boutique fantasque*.

His companion thought of *L'Apprenti sorcier* — the young person in the ballet fingering everything until he did some irreversible thing that set it all in motion, awoke it to life, and told the tale on him. This was about to be fulfilled.

On a bureau was a small, delicate pair of scales — for weighing letters? He touched one scale, pressed down the diminutive plate with one finger. It wouldn't come back! Nothing that he could do would rectify it: it remained stuck.

That would tell its tale to the returning master of it all: he would have no difficulty in interpreting it. The objects themselves would speak in a hundred voices, wooden or metallic, of what these two had been up to, the irruption into their privacy, the rape of their virginity.

*

In some panic they fled. Back into the first room — the drawers so carefully stuffed with matches and lighters; a bicycle lamp and all the accessories for clerical bicycling.

Hardly a moment left for the pictures, the crowded photographs that spoke for the repressed heart: in those confined, constricted rooms, so packed one had to thread one's way through the ordered maze — yet the photograhs spoke of exalted landscapes, mountains, snow peaks, pine forests, great faraway lakes.

Now the November sunlight flooded in at full, blue shadows under the wall of the Garden Court and along the rose-terrace — filling those overcrowded, walled-up rooms with a sense of emptiness, desolation. For the one thing missing — and all was designed perhaps to shore him up from missing — was Love.

*

Silent, oppressed, amazed by the revelation they had received

38

and by the sadness of it all, they stole down the staircase and out into the Garden Court. Here they could breathe at last.

*

They had paid their visit just in time. For, shortly afterwards, the Chaplain made his decision.

Retiring from being Steward, he would retire from the Chaplaincy also. He did not wish to remain on under 'that man' in any capacity.

And, of course, 'that man' lost the collection of silver and the pictures which he had so much desired for the institution he ruled.

Handsombody accepted the offer that came from his original college where he had been an undergraduate, and there the collection remains as a great ornament — though few have heard of it — to this day.

IV

Naboth's Vineyard

The young man had several Naboth's Vineyards, as he called them to himself, in Cornwall — though he was not Cornish. In fact he was half-American, his father having been a painter of some distinction, though not recognised, who worked along with the Newlyn School of painters in the halcyon days before 1914 signalled the end of the old European civilisation.

It was then that the son, Michael, developed a perfect fixation upon Cornwall, from holidays along the coast — paradise to him away from the boredom of school.

He explored for himself, taking sketch book along with him, following in father's footsteps, with less gift, less promise. Given to day-dreaming, he was something of a *fantaisiste*, building fantasies around the particular places, the houses, he fancied.

They certainly had something special about them — tribute to his taste at least.

One of them, Trevillick, had a marvellous situation by a south-flowing river, tidal up to the point where the grey church tower was reflected in still waters, which lapped the edge of the churchyard. And the house above it! — just what he fancied: not too big for a bachelor, a Queen Anne front with long windows that looked sideways down to where the estuary took a curve, disguising the harbour mouth some miles beyond. A pretty neat sward before it, summer-house at the side: all very inviting for sitting out, sketching the moods and colours of river and sky.

Alas, the house was a vicarage, occupied by an incumbent
— Michael thought the word appropriate in the circumstances: no hope of it.

Another of his Naboth's Vineyards was incumbed upon by
the Church too. This was a sequestered inland place at the
head of a valley of rocks. The ancient little rectory had been
added to in good Georgian days, in the silvery granite of the
moors above. It occupied an enchanting hollow, sheltered by
a line of beeches above.

Alas, the incumbent was still spry: no hope of outing him,
or the Church — as yet.

Michael thought there was more hope of his third fixation, a
place inland from the North coast — as indeed there was, for
it was not in mortmain, in the dead hand of the Church. The
house belonged to an ancient West Country family that had a
larger place in Devon, and hardly ever visited it, but leased it
to a succession of tenants, who came and went rather rapidly
— no suspicion, however, attached.

The house lay on the ridge above a deep rift, dark with
evergreens. Though the windows of the front were Georgian,
a practised eye could see from the buttresses that the struc-
ture was much earlier, represented a Tudor hall. The eighteenth century part ran back some way in depth, lateral
windows looking out easterly, to a large servants' hall at the
back — admirable for a studio with its northern light.

While Michael was away at school tenants at Treneglos
succeeded each other: none registered except a City of
London man, a knight, who made an impression by going
bankrupt. No one expected that.

The absentee owners, having had enough trouble over
tenants and the lease, eventually decided to sell. Sale oddly
held fire.

Some time elapsed, when Michael came into his inheritance
from an East Anglian grandmother — Elizabethan house,

small estate, pedigree herd of cattle. What would he do with a pedigree herd? Without a moment's hesitation he sold the lot, and bought his Naboth's Vineyard.

He was in a seventh heaven of delight — no diminution of it that the old house was now in some disrepair and needed attending to. That added further interest: he could tinker with it to his heart's content, rearrange rooms, fixtures, paint it up to his own taste.

Now he could live his own life as all along he had meant to do. When an Oxford friend of his invited him up for a week-end to enjoy the fleshpots of All Saints College, Michael replied simply:

'I have no intention of ever crossing the Tamar again.'

His friend thought it rather odd of him, but then Cornwall gets some people like that.

Michael found that he had on hand rather more than he bargained for. But in the neighbouring hamlet he found a wonderful helper, an elderly carpenter who was a gifted craftsman with the soul of an artist. He could make a pan-elled door after a Georgian pattern, an oval table with horse-hoof legs, and also do the expert polishing.

Arthur, wild head of busy white hair, red cheeks, small twinkling eyes, didn't talk much, but what he did say meant more than appeared, in the indirect sly manner of a native Cornishman. There was an instinctive understanding between the two artists, and Michael found himself relying on his car-penter friend for information as to the history of the house.

Why so many quick changes of tenancy? — Now that he was in possession he had no intention of giving up, the place was his for good and all.

But what was what about it?

One of the intervening tenants — was it the knight who had gone bankrupt? — had made some changes that neither Michael nor his friend approved of.

A clinkered tennis court disturbed the slope in front of the house.

'There will be no tennis while I am here,' Michael declared. 'Too much else to do.'

The two of them would dislodge a few of the clinkers, pop in a cutting — fuchsia, hydrangea, veronica — anything would take here, and shortly a garden was under way.

Similarly with the swimming pool to the west of the house. Michael thought it unsightly, wrong for an old Cornish manor house. 'A stockbroker's dream,' he declared. Anyway he couldn't swim — and there would be no Lido while he held sway.

The cavity made a convenient spot for laying up logs and branches they brought in from the spinney, sheltered too for sawing up wood for the huge open hearth in the hall/studio at the back of the house.

*

It was some time before Michael noticed the curious behaviour of a feature by which he set special store. Among its attractions was a solid old staircase of black oak with a dog-gate at the foot. Michael liked that, though he had no dog: it spoke to him of the Georgian past and keeping the farm dogs from trespassing upstairs.

Eventually, however, he did notice that at times when he had shut it behind him at night, in the morning it was wide open. Had he remembered aright? Had he in fact closed it?

Rather absent-minded, he could not be sure. He decided to keep notice, keep watch — really *on himself*.

Sure enough, one morning after he had carefully closed it and made note that he fastened it, it was wide open again.

Had anyone passed up or down?

There was no one sleeping in the house but himself, his Spartan wants were attended to by the carpenter's wife from the hamlet, Treneglos Vean.

So one day he mentioned to her casually what he had noticed and asked her what she thought.

'I dare say 'tes the wind, sir, surely.' He noticed a rather evasive look in her eye; then she added, 'Ben't it?'

He did not feel so sure, so he asked the carpenter himself. He too said something about the wind blowing it open.

This added a further chore: Michael tried to check whether the unexplained opening of the dog-gate was confined to windy nights. Again he could not be sure.

Talking with Arthur he learned something of the Cornish folklore about Jan Tregagle, and how the old servants would say, when the winter wind blew down the great chimney upon the open hearth, 'Tha's Jan Tregagle roarin'.' Or, when the wind howled in the back court: 'There 'e is 'owlin for 'is sins.'

So Tregagle was a wind-spirit.

But what had that to do with the Treneglos dog-gate? Michael left the question — unlike the gate — open.

Then there was the curious matter of the clock. Michael purchased a fine example of a grandfather clock, from the firm with the celebrated name of Button, Menhenitt and Mutton.

This was a masterpiece of the no less celebrated clock-maker, Roger Wearne, whose headstone of a century-and-a-half ago may still be seen in the churchyard at his native St Erth, with a rhyming inscription about his now keeping time to all eternity.

His clock had never been known to fail; but now it was behaving oddly. Michael treated it with great respect, wound up its heavy weights carefully and with conscientious regularity.

But when he descended the staircase, through his dog-gate, to breakfast Roger Wearne's masterpiece would be telling him it was 3.20. Michael went regularly to bed, like the poet Auden, at 9 p.m.; when the clock would be saying, most improbably, 2.30. Was it laughing at him?

He had it inspected by a great authority on clocks, the local vicar, who reported nothing wrong mechanically.

Then what was?

Was it the wind again, or Jan Tregagle?

The disused swimming-pool, wood-store, sawpit, or whatever, at length raised a question in Michael's mind, now alerted.

Anyone who works among trees knows the occasional, shockingly human sound that a tree, or the rubbing of two branches against each other in the wind, will give forth — one starts as if one hears a human cry, looks up, around — as if someone. . . .

No wonder there has been so much ancient lore about humans being turned into trees, or imprisoned in trees — as Prospero imprisoned Caliban's mother, Sycorax.

Well, occasionally, when Michael was coming to the end of his stint of sawing in the wood-pit, in twilight at the close of day, darkness encroaching, he fancied that he distinctly heard a groan. Did he hear it? Or did he fancy it?

He made up his mind to ask the carpenter, to tackle him directly — no more evasions — if there was a story. If so, what was it?

Then, and only then, Arthur 'up and told' him, as we say.

There was a story. It went back to the bankrupt knight's brief tenancy. There had been an uproarious, rowdy, noisy party in the great hall at the back of the house. A fellow, a stranger who had been brought in to wait, stepped outside that night for a moment and into the pool. Was he tight? Anyway, he couldn't swim. With so much noise and uproar, nobody heard anything; nor, in such a crowd, was he missed.

A macabre detail the carpenter — typically Cornish — added. When the body was picked up in the morning, the toes of his patent shoes were worn through with scraping to get a toehold on the cement wall.

45

One way and another Michael's 'Naboth's Vineyard' was giving him food for thought, rather more than he had bargained for.

On a dun November afternoon he was sitting in the long panelled front room giving on the terrace, the louring light of day's end in keeping with his thoughts: What *was* strange about the house? How to account for these curious, disparate happenings? He felt the hairs on his neck rising, a slight shiver, when the front door-bell suddenly rang.

He went to the door and opened it, to find a strange lady in grey, unknown to him. But what gave him a shock were her words; quite simply she said:

'Can you tell me, is this house haunted?'

V

The Pinetum

What an extraordinary atmosphere the pinetum had! In itself it was a rarity on the south coast of Cornwall, where conifers are not indigenous. It was a monument to the enterprise – and not only the enterprise – of the man who had planted it over a hundred years ago.

There was indeed something architectural about it. It was quite square, bounded to the north by a wall, beyond which were the considerable kitchen gardens and establishment a country mansion demanded in those days. Within the large rectangle – something like a College court at Cambridge – he had marked out pathways, all converging upon a monument erected in the middle: pivot of the place, which somehow gave meaning to it. The clever young grandson of the lodge-keeper, at the bottom of the drive leading up across the park, could never make out what. Anyhow, he was not supposed to penetrate it.

As a boy, inquisitive as all Cornish folk are, he sometimes ventured into the formal Italian garden below the terrace of the big house. Even here he was not supposed to be – but who would stop him? For the house was shut up, deserted by the family, guarded only by an ancient retainer behind the shuttered windows. However, if he peeped out around a half-opened shutter, he was not very spry.

Once the boy penetrated beyond, to the edge of the pinetum. To his imagination it was a cathedral: over-arching vaults, green glooms; vistas like aisles of a church, at the end a ray of sunlight as if from transept or clerestory window, making the gloom within all the more lugubrious, positively sinister. At the crossing he caught a glimpse of a stone monument.

Above all, was the overpowering smell of the pinetum, aromatic, resinous, sleep-inducing like a drug. At the nearer edge was a border of box, and that scent — so idiosyncratic, so nostalgic as to be almost mnemonic — he did not like. Thenceforth he kept away.

He did not know that among the various sorts of pines — stone pines, umbrella pines, giant macrocarpa, larches, firs, marsh-cypress, and even a Montezuma pine from Mexico — there was indeed a sleep-inducing tree, which could act as a drug: a rare kind of sassafras, which the early colonists of Virginia thought to be a cure for syphilis.

Nor did the boy know till much later the story of the visiting lady from a neighbouring estate in the Glyn Valley, who had come to visit the pinetum in an earlier stage of its growth. The lady, on a hot summer afternoon, had called out her carriage, and driven over to inspect the progress of the pinetum. Much impressed by the rare variety of sassafras, she had taken a branch with her into the close atmosphere of the carriage.

Arrived back at her own house, she could not get out. The coachman was at a loss: he had never known his lady, a rather formidable dowager, in this condition before. A faint? — she had never been known to faint. A stroke, perhaps? Her physician, conveniently at hand, was summoned, and pronounced:

'An extraordinary thing — her ladyship's drunk.'

She was put to bed, in a bemused condition, unable to give a coherent account of herself; but, drunk she was not. She had been overcome, on a hot day, enclosed in her carriage with the overpowering fumes of the sassafras.

*

The family itself was peculiar enough, as the lodge-keeping boy gradually learned when he grew up — not wholly with sympathy, more with a mixture of fascination, envy, and exasperation.

For they had been rich, with all the revenues and dues coming in from the mines upon their lands, at the heyday of Cornish mining in the mid-nineteenth century. Then the last squire of the elder line, after a raffish career in the Army, brought back a mistress, with whom he lived as man and wife, and produced a family which learned that it was illegitimate only upon his death.

They were thunderstruck, and no less resentful. He had taken as much money as he could out of the entailed estate to provide for them. The estate itself came to the next heirs, the family of his brother, who — even less promising — had been sent off years before, as a kind of remittance man, ranching in Montana.

The brother had had a family of three sons and a daughter. But the first two of these were illegitimate too, so the inheritance was to come to the youngest son, who — to prepare him to take it up and accustom him to the ways of the old country — was sent home to school, and then on to Cambridge. Oddly again, exceptionally for a West Country family, they had a tradition of going to Cambridge from the eighteenth century. What residual ability there was in the family rested in the girl, who accompanied her brother to England. A few years older, she was the dominant partner, who took him in tow, and managed his affairs.

She could not always be on the spot, however: she had her own life to run and, a strong-minded woman, she made a 'good' marriage. The rather reprobate males of the family were apt to boast that they married their cooks. They had certainly left a penumbra of illegitimates about the purlieus of the estate. And the brother, Piers, managed to escape his sister's surveillance when he went up from school to a brief residence at the university.

*

These events preceded the lodge-keeper's grandson's growing up. In those days faithful retainers could be trusted to keep the family secrets to themselves, and anyway below-stairs gossip rarely penetrated the true nature of events.

A kind of hiatus prevailed in the family history — the growing boy saw it through the romantic aura of the historical novels that were his favourite reading. The last squire to live up at the big house had died some years before — the next heir was a boy at school.

The house was shut up, shutters closed — only occasionally opened to let in a little light and air, by the ancient butler, marooned there like a servitor of some traditional cult with its rites: opening, or half-opening, and closing the shutters in front (he lived at the back of the big house).

Every quarter there descended upon the sleeping place the sister, Regina, now a formidable and titled dowager. Her visits coincided with the rent-days, the manor-court or court-baron held in the large upstairs assembly-room of the estate-inn, the Penvanson Arms: a male gathering, which then sat down to the traditional dinner, enormous barons of roast beef under their covers, presided over by the steward.

Her ladyship was not present — but her presence was felt in the background. She represented the family: she gave the orders, was the final court of appeal. She kept her secret, or rather, her brother's, to herself. Only occasionally at the lodge-gate, her retainer's grandson never once glimpsed her.

Not often seen on the place, she was something of a legend, and stories were told of her. Her recluse of a brother was easy-going and careless; she, on her visits, was a regular tartar.

One morning she ordered the carriage too early for the

red-faced, boss-eyed coachman, who overslept himself after a midnight carouse.

There being no time to make the vehicle presentable, he washed clean only one side of it, that which he drew up at the portico to take her in — in both senses of the word.

She was not taken in; he was sacked on the spot.

This story the lodgekeeping boy did learn from his grandfather — faithful to the family, not one to divulge much of what he knew of them, whom he had helped to carry to the grave, including the last.

Below-stairs gossip, never very subtle or at all penetrating, said that he had died of 'a broken heart'. He was indeed a bachelor — why had he never married, done his duty to carry on the line?

The very knowing ones among the former servants — females of course — said that he had been rejected by the daughter of a neighbouring family. This was incomprehensible: he was a good match: the estate was one of the best in the neighbourhood, farms, coverts, house-property in the county town, ground-rents of shops in Plymouth. Who would have the face to refuse him?

The hearts of old-time female servants — an extinct species — were incurably romantic.

*

The young lad at the lodge-gate was of a different make, and generation. He wanted to know the truth. And one day, years later, he was admitted into the deserted house, and into its last occupant's inner sanctum: a rather gloomy smoking room, with a backgammon closet, looking out upon the eighteenth-century cockpit and across to the pinetum.

The room had a bookcase of late Victorian novels, not very inspiring to look into. But when he did look in, he was at first nonplussed to see the word *Nihil* written in at the last page of every one of them. He thought at first that the word applied solely to the book — as one might say today, 'No good'. But with the unvarying rejection of each one and everything, he felt a sudden intuition that he had looked into a dead man's heart, who had found life empty.

Again, why?

Grown-up now, he was in a position to pursue his researches further.

He found that the melancholy bachelor — he felt a kind of kinship with the dead man whose soul he had looked into — was no rejected suitor of the neighbouring squire's daughter: he had never summoned up courage, or whatever, to make a proposal.

On coming down from the university, he had pursued a solitary life, never going abroad, shutting himself up on the estate, rarely going outside it. He gave himself up to planting — not only the pinetum but the fringes of rhododendrons that marked the boundary of the estate along the main road, that drew exclamations of delight at their purple glory from travellers along it, long after he was dead.

He would appear to have been a misogynist. For the maids in the house had strict orders not to be seen when he was about, or ever to meet him on stairs, or in corridor or passage.

He had an attendant, a man-servant whom he had brought down with him from Cambridge, who knew his ways and had the key to his wants.

A still more faithful attendant, in fact inseparable, was his dog Fido, who lived with him day and night. A faithful black labrador, with those wonderful brown eyes full of love and understanding — unlike the sad, hopeless eyes of cattle foreknowing their fate — the dog was in constant attendance all day and every day, at the tree planting, selecting and sorting and weeding, which was the Master's main occupation.

Almost his only occupation. Sometimes there had to be a

shoot on the place. Regina swept down from her London home to be hostess for her bachelor brother. Solely a man's party; loads of pasties baked in the kitchen, to be carried out hot to the guns. Fido was trained to take no part in the pursuit of the birds: he remained with his Master, who was relieved when it was all over, the bare minimum of duty to the county done.

At length the favourite dog died.

The Master was distraught. For a time he took interest in having a likeness of the dog sculpted in stone and erected at the crossing in the pinetum, where he could just glimpse it from his smoking room. A fine figure of a dog, seated with a twist of shoulder, just as he would turn to look up into the Master's face.

The man himself sank into deeper melancholy. No more shooting-parties, no more anything: *Nihil*.

The family weakness − besides that for illegitimacy, or marrying (if at all) the cook − was drink. This grew upon Piers.

Frightened maids would overhear an altercation between him and his man:

'James! James! Bring me a bottle of whisky.'

'No − you shan't have it.'

'James! You hear me. I must have it.'

'No. You know the doctor's orders, sir.'

'Damn all the doctors! What good have they ever done for me?'

James was silent. It was too true. But he would not give way.

And what were the pieces of wadding, the cotton-wool pads, the maids would find casually thrown into the smoking-room fireplace?

Little did they know, in their country innocence.

*

The searching mind of the old lodge-keeper's grandson

found out what the grandfather had never known — or had he? — the explanation.

At the university Piers had slept one night with a prostitute, and contracted the most appalling syphilis, then incurable. This had ruined his life.

One night, not so long after the monument to the favourite dog was finished, he took his gun out and there beside it, shot himself.

VI

After Sixty Years

Kellow's shop was the hub of the universe at the cross-roads at the upper end of our long straggling china-clay village. Very conveniently placed for trade it was, a grocers' and general store. And, no less conveniently, old man Kellow had half-a-dozen up-and-coming daughters to help in the shop. A very good thing they had made of it: they did a roaring trade, an old-fashioned family concern in those days before multiple shops and super-markets.

A fine lot of girls they were, from the eldest, Harriet, to the young twins, Ellen and Gwen. They all had personality too, something of the spirit of their fiery father − a forceful man, who ruled all in that busy heaving household with a ready hand, an impatient temper.

That shop was always full of people, one of the girls behind the counter on either side, the sharp old man − as he appeared to me, a mere boy, in the background. Of course, I never knew what went on in that dark interior. For that I am indebted to my foxy old Uncle Mark, who observed everything with those glinting grey eyes of his.

The twins were a great source of attraction to a bright one among the young commercial travellers. After doing his business, and even before, he would be flirting with them. Business over, Mr Kellow − he was always 'Mr' to the villagers − would say: 'Now then, young man: I'm going to town. We'll be able to go down together.' So off they went.

On the way down the young man − up to that one − would say, 'Well, good-bye: I've got to call in at Mrs R.'s' − the little sweet-shop which made no such fortune as Mr Kellow's up along. As soon as the old boy was round the corner out of sight the breezy traveller would race back to go on with the girls.

A younger commercial was so nervous that he wouldn't go back to town in the dark — down that elmy, rustling long lane, past the turnings at kissing-gates — unless someone went with him. (Neither would we — there was something awesome about those turnings at that lonely spot below the village.) Two of the girls used to have to accompany him down as far as that spot and see him safely past it. No lights to lighten the darkness then.

O the simplicity of those days! *O sancta simplicitas!*

*

Harriet, at sixteen, was much taken with Phil Richards, of just her age — they had gone to school together, along the road, from the time they were children. Up and up they had gone — hand in hand, you might say — from standard to standard until they reached the top and left school together when barely fourteen. A great bond.

One of Mr Kellow's absolute rules — and that disciplinarian had several by which to keep order in his large menagerie — was that you had to be indoors by 9.30 p.m. You were all right up to 9.30, but a minute later by his gold repeater — and you were for it.

One fine evening, when Harriet and Phil had been out for a walk together, they were a few minutes late in returning. Father was outside on the doorstep, watch in hand — an impatient man. He slapped Harriet's face smartly, and gave Phil a swift kick in the pants.

'Come back in seven years,' he said.

Phil slunk submissively down the steps, out into the road. He never came back.

*

For those two young people it was the end of an idyll.

They had spent the evening up at the Carn, the pile of flat altar-shaped rocks high up above the straggling village, which dominated all that landscape for miles. From there views extended in every direction: out over the bay and the Gribbin headland, curiously foreshortened at such a height; away to the west, Hensbarrow, the 'old' barrow that marked the grave of some prehistoric chief hereabouts. In the east Brown Willy and Rowtor on the Horizon; in the nearer distance across Sterrick Moor the grey tower of Luxulyan church, the westering sun lighting up the western face.

It was a haunted place, made for dedication, or sacrifice.

As they sat there on the rock, looking out over miles on miles of their homeland, the bells of Luxulyan began to ring in the distance — practice-night for the ringers. Then and there, to the changing sound of church-bells, sometimes sounding clear and near, then faint and far, the young couple exchanged their first kiss: a kind of pledge.

One way and another they never forgot that evening, or its abrupt ending.

*

They grew up, and lived their lives apart. He never moved away from his home town. Harriet married away and went to live at Plymouth. A strong personality, she coupled up with a man she could respect, who was up to her. They had a house full of children — seven sons. She had a full life, plenty of work and outside interests; she could be said to have had a happy — certainly a fulfilled — life, with ups and downs, events to fill it out, one way and another.

Phil had not. He had somehow acquired a wife, a woman of no personality or interest. He himself had none. A certain amount of money came to him from the family business — no need to exert himself. Nor did he. After that an annuity came in. They had no children.

*

During the war this couple, now in their seventies, came to live with Uncle Mark, who had married one of the Kellow sisters. Phil and his wife occupied one of the two large front rooms — and never moved from the fireside. Phil lived in his carpet slippers, and never stirred out so much as to go up the road to the old shop, long ago taken over and no such hub of activity now.

But Harriet's sister knew that Phil would like to see her again, before death took him. He had become a complete valetudinarian, concerned with nothing much in the world save his health.

*

One day Harriet came. Her sister had a word with her in her front room.

'You'd like to see Phil, wouldn't you?'

The sister went across to Phil's room:

'You'd like to see Harriet, wouldn't you?'

'Come in along' — this to Harriet, standing outside.

She had become a large, rather formidable woman, accustomed to being treated with deference by the other sisters as the eldest. And her life had been full of incident, some blows with such a large family; but she had risen above them.

As the girl Phil remembered she had had a long roll of corn-gold hair down her back. Now it was piled on top of her head — it gave her an air of authority — now white with only a glint of corn.

Phil saw her enter, with more than a touch of dismay, and began excusing himself, his appearance, etc. Seeing no

response, he fell back on, 'Well, Harriet, how is it with you?
. . . You see how it is with me — I've had a lot of poor
health. . . . If you've been in poor health a good many years,
you don't feel up to much . . . up to facing things, I mean,
Harriet.' He repeated the name, lingering over it — as he had
often lingered over it in his mind in the years between.

Harriet's sister thought — 'a poor fish' — then shut the
door, leaving them together.

*

They hadn't seen each other since that evening sixty years
ago. It was present in both their minds unspoken. They were
now old people, life nearly over.

What he wanted more than anything was to regain her
respect, lost by his submissive acceptance of his dismissal by
her father, with never an effort to come back at him, sur-
mount it.

Perhaps it was his own self-respect that he had lost and
wanted, at this last moment, to regain. Who knows whether
it had not gone for something in breaking his confidence in
himself?

He wanted now — going back to boyhood — for her to
take his acheing head in her arms and rest it there — as if
for ever.

That last evening so long ago was present in both their
minds: the sharp visual clarity everything seems to have when
one is young — an ache at the heart to remember it; the blue
distances, larks singing over the downs, the bells ringing
nearer, then farther; the senses sharpened by youth and first
love; scent of heather and young bracken and camomile.
They had looked down into the quarry-pool together and
thrown stones, breaking their reflections in the water —
unlucky, Harriet had said.

And now this was how life had been for both of them. Life

59

was nearly over — had long been over for him — indeed, he had never lived.

It was a bitter moment for him. Perhaps, with her beside him, he might have made more of a success of it? Could he have been a different man, with her spirit? All the girls of that family had spirit and courage and pride.

Now, there remained only the unspoken need to justify himself in her eyes.

She saw him without illusions. Sixty years ago it had hurt her pride that he had had so little spirit. To take her father's dismissal of him without a word!

'Come back in seven years!' — a fellow with any pride would have found a way of coming back in seven days. From Phil, never a word. And the smarts of youth mean so much more than later.

But she was a girl of spirit. She went on, and at length found her man — a man who could lay down the framework for their joint lives, had given her children — seven of them, all sons — and provide for them. A successful working partnership.

She looked at, and through, this earlier memory without giving any sign — unmoving, it seemed. She had gone through a lot in life; it had hardened her. He had softened.

He found her daunting — he could not find his way back to the girl he had known, whose memory had remained untarnished all these years.

He went on, faltering, propitiatingly: 'We had no children. Now if only we had had children. . . .'

Harriet spoke: 'They bring their troubles.' He only then remembered that she had had two of her sons killed in the war.

Phil said softly: 'Yes. You've had your troubles too.'

There was a sound of footsteps coming downstairs — in a moment his wife would be here — they'd be no longer alone. He saw the old spirit gleam in her eye that had so much

60

attracted him, and suddenly she took the grizzled head in her hands and gave him a swift, deliberate kiss.

The footsteps approached, a hand on the door handle, and slowly the wife came in.

VII

His Reverence

They called him 'his Reverence' in the parish — not out of
respect, I fancy, nor precisely out of disrespect. For he was
the well-to-do Rector of a good farming parish, a scion of an
old county family with means of his own, and those were
Edwardian days when one's betters were recognised. It was a
tribute to his importance, which bordered on the portentous,
and was only slightly equivocal.

For there was something equivocal about him — his personality and circumstances suggested that; the cause not
known or guessed at, certainly not by his clerical neighbours.

He looked formidable, with his bushy black beard, in those
days when his colleagues went mostly clean-shaven. Then too
he had a habit of peering out over his steely spectacles, when
addressing some censorious words — usually as to morals —
to his congregation.

Perhaps censoriousness was the tone of the Rectory and he
took it from his acidulated spinster sister, who kept house for
him. That and rather ill-natured gossip were the expressions
of art her nature allowed her — or perhaps the forms her
sexual repression took. Rather curious in the circumstances
of the Rectory.

These were distinctly well-heeled, and allowed the Rector
to keep a carriage and pair, when most of his colleagues
walked, or pedalled around their parishes on bicycles — for
those were the great days when bicycling came in. Indeed, a

famous cleric of the time gave voice to the new excitement, in
verse: 'Going Downhill on a Bicycle':

> Swifter and yet more swift,
> Till the heart with a mighty lift
> Makes the lungs laugh, the throat cry:
> 'O bird, see; see, bird, I fly.'

None of that for the Rector: it would have been contrary to
his dignity, which was considerable.

So was his state within doors. Oil-lamps in hall and corridor; silver candlesticks and salvers in the dining room. A
good table was kept; for the Rector liked his food, and had a
bright eye for a nubile girl, in Bible class or Sunday School.

But he was without wife to comfort his bed.

Why?

The fact was that he had had a wife, an attractive woman
years younger than himself, but she had left him. She was not
Cornish, and it was understood that she did not like country
life in that remote and primitive county. She was a Londoner
— in itself a suspicious circumstance: anything might be
expected from that quarter, particularly anything flighty.
The fact that she had taken flight from the Rector confirmed
their suspicions — and won him the chief measure of sympathy, the only warmth, he enjoyed.

Or, perhaps, it was not quite the only warmth.

For, some years before, while his wife still lived with him,
there had come into the parish a retired farming family, with
a buxom daughter of some thirty or so, still unmarried.

There is no accounting for tastes, still less for the secrets of
the marriage bed — it may be that his pretty wife was cold,
she certainly gave him no children — but the Rector preferred the warmer bosom of the lower-class newcomer to his
lady-like wife from London.

Clandestine meetings took place.

In village life there is always one pair of eyes that lives for the excitement of spying on their neighbours, particularly their sexual misdemeanours, innocent — or barely nocent — pleasures. Anyway, nobody else's business. But hammer-chinned, witch-like Eliza made it wholly her business: a dedicated soul, keeping watch with a twitch of her bedroom curtains in the evenings, or out to pick up sticks in the lanes by night. And her cottage was conveniently close to the back entrance to the Rectory.

Such was her obsession, she might today be regarded as a *voyeur* — or is there such a word as *voyeuse*? It was a female occupation anyway and, in the event, well rewarded.

Up in the Rectory glebe was a haycock, which provided a comfortable bed for assignations; the Rector and the buxom newcomer made considerable use of it. But not without Eliza's malevolent knowledge. For the present she said nothing; she awaited the inevitable consequence — for though avoidable, it was inevitable.

The Rector's wife, enclosed within her airs and graces, was unaware. But one night the truth broke upon her.

The Rector had taken advantage of the absence of his lover's parents to pay a visit to her house, where her bedroom at the back, under the sloping roof, had no very high drop to the ground. The Rector made an enjoyably, a risky, long stay of it — and before midnight the parents returned.

Hurriedly dressing, but minus his trousers, he made his escape, nimbly down from that low back window. A pair of athletic legs glinted in the moonlight as they made their way back between the laurels of the Rectory drive.

History does not relate what the young woman did with those clerical trousers. But a friend of the historian once heard two cockney women confiding secrets to each other on top of a London bus, and one said awesomely to the other:

'It was the button-hook that opened her eyes.'

It was the Rector's trouserless state that opened his wife's eyes. There was no accounting for *that*.

Thereupon she took herself off, back to London — with a well-paid allowance.

It was as well that the Rector had private means, for there were other accounts to settle too. But it meant that, now, he could not afford to give up his living. Just when things hung in the balance, almost over the edge, he had to hang on, like a man half way down a cliff.

For, of course, the farmer's daughter proved pregnant — the worst of the lower classes was that their women were so pregnable, when his upper-class wife, with her superior airs, gave him no offspring. Ticklish as his situation was, he rather liked the thought of having a child of his own, and hoped it would be a son.

But the girl — woman, rather — was to be provided for.

How did he manage in this crisis, this thunderclap when all things came together?

His family pride, or arrogance — brazenness, call it what you will — helped him out; his coolness saw him through. But it took some courage.

In those days a clergyman could not divorce, and re-marry — particularly when he was the guilty party. Nor, in truth, with his family background and kin among half — or at least a quarter — of the local gentry — would he have married his 'fancy woman', as the pretty phrase went.

She took off on a long visit to relations in Canada — in reality to a maternity home, where she produced a son, to the Rector's satisfaction.

She did not return. Her parents moved away — which solved one problem. The Rector set up a home for her in a South Coast resort — not too far away for convenience, yet outside the West Country. And this made a convenient home away from home for his holidays. That solved the second problem.

Next, domestic arrangements at the Rectory had to be provided for. The Rector had some difficulty in recalling his sister to keep house for him. Truth was, she had disliked the intrusion of a young wife from London — no connexions in the county, no family to speak of. She was even more of a snob than her brother — would never have demeaned *her*self by falling for one of the lower orders. (Nor would one of them have been likely to fall for her.)

But she had to be squared. Henceforth she had a hold over her brother; she held to it and extended it. No man is a hero to his own valet; still less to his housekeeper. Within the Rectory she returned to rule the roost — and had a large say in ruling the parish too. Gossip was her outlet, her recreation, her foible. But never a word passed her lips as to what had happened, or what the situation really was.

She allowed it to be understood that her brother had been badly treated by his wife: a case of desertion. As the years grew and the situation became fixed, taken for granted, a certain amount of sympathy for the Rector grew. No one questioned the rather lengthy holidays he took away from home.

There remained Eliza to be dealt with. She knew of the assignations on the comfortable haycock, had had ocular evidence, and no difficulty in putting two and two together, when both Rector's wife and farmer's daughter disappeared.

A pound a week for life settled her hash, and made her sit cosy in her cottage. Her hammer-chin closed on her remittance: nothing could be got out of her when neighbours spoke of the change at the Rectory.

Thus were all the problems solved, the situation satisfactorily fixed and congealed.

It had been a close thing, and needed nerve. Nerve to confront his mistress's parents, fix things up with them and her. Nerve to pass Eliza's cottage day by day; it took some time before he felt sure that she would not tattle. However, a pound a week made sure:

'Better'n Lloyd George', she said to herself — it was the time when Lloyd George got all the credit with country folk for introducing old-age pensions. Those were five bob a week; Eliza was doing far better.

Oddly enough, most nerve was needed to deal with the sister, and fix her. She held the master-key to the situation — if she had been unwilling to come in on it the Rector's position would have been much weaker. She guaranteed it, made all respectable and square; and, for her, running the Rectory and half the parish was a career. She had her position in the county.

The Rector was able to confront his duties, eventually with renewed confidence and authority: he ruled his flock and ordered them about, censored their shortcomings, particularly moral — and 'moral' in the country meant only one thing; he preached at them, rather than to them; he christened them, married and buried them.

He fulfilled his duties; thus, and from his family position, he was regarded with some deference by the clerical families of the neighbourhood. Though not so flush with money as he had been, nor so much given to entertaining, he was able to patronise them quite a bit. His sister did her duty, not only as patroness of the Mother's Union, but assiduously giving and attending neighbourly bridge-parties.

Since he had so active a deputy in social matters, and as years passed he could still afford to engage a curate, his holidays away grew more and more lengthy. As he aged, somewhat prematurely, his sister gave out that this was on the score of his health.

In fact, away from home, he had a rather satisfactory home-life, such as he never had enjoyed at the Rectory. And he was quite besotted on his son, who promised to combine the self-confidence of the father with the engaging complacency and willingness of the mother. When the Rector died, still comparatively warm, his will revealed that he had left everything to his unknown son.

It was only then that the scandal broke. Great was the indignation, particularly among the ladies, in the rectories, and perhaps especially in the vicarages, which he had patronised. They felt themselves deceived — worse, made fools of. Censoriousness had a fine fling for a while; moreover, the tale carried an immoral moral — so far from virtue being rewarded, ill-conduct and deception all round had come off rather well. No sermon could get round that.

However, the sensation was short-lived. The Rector's demise, and the revelation from his will, came in the midst of the 1914—1918 war, when people had other things to think of.

The last words were spoken by Eliza, and they were characteristically ungrateful:

'To think I've bin and shut me mouth all they years!'

VIII

The Room above the Cloisters

What is there in the atmosphere of a room? There must be *something* — so many people are aware of it and sensitive to it. Especially if there has been an experience of great unhappiness suffered within it. It seems to be a passive experience that registers and leaves some aura in the atmosphere, as if clinging to the walls.

Once, indeed, I have heard of a room that radiated happiness — to such an extent that it healed the breach between a couple whose marriage was foundering. This was the case of the upstairs bedroom of the Virginian novelist, Ellen Glasgow, at her house quite celebrated in its day, No. 1, Main Street, Richmond, Va.

But what are we to think of the rather macabre record of a set of rooms over the south wing of the cloisters, in an old cathedral city in the west of England?

They were a very desirable set, with a large sitting room, panelled in oak just before the disastrous Civil War that did so much damage to the Cathedral, a little study for books besides, and upstairs a largeish bedroom with fine semicircular roof-beam arching above the bed. Both sitting-room and bedroom had a good southerly aspect looking down the slope, above the huddle of ancient roofs and chimneys, to the river at the foot and away to a crest of woods in the distance.

So that these rooms were much in request in the College of Vicars-choral, of which they formed part — and also were a cause of heart-burning among those members who aspired to occupy them.

Occupation, however, went by seniority, unless the next on the rota happened to be a married man with a house in the city, or a bachelor who was prepared to waive his turn for another, or simply didn't want to occupy the set for some reason of his own.

*

Towards the end of the Victorian age these rooms were occupied by an elderly vicar-choral, who was always known as 'the Professor'. In earlier years he had been a professor of music in some small institution, and the awkward air of a professor had stuck to him.

He was a small man, weak and wizened, considerate of others to such an extent that people regarded him as totally ineffective. Out of consideration for others in the cloisters, he had installed a soundless keyboard on which he practised Bach's Preludes and Fugues. He had in fact written a standard work on the subject.

At the regular Audit meetings of the College, which dealt with its affairs, he was accustomed to being ridden roughshod over by the very competent Treasurer, who conducted its business. He had a sharp edge to his tongue, and would say with an air of concluding any discussion of an awkward problem:

'I don't suppose that the Professor wants to prolong discussion of this matter.'

Or, 'I don't suppose that the Professor has any contribution to make on this thorny question.'

Or even, 'I don't think we need bother Mr Chapman for his opinion.'

But one day the worm turned − and certainly turned the tables on his persecutor. He rose, and said at the end of the Audit:

'I know that my opinion doesn't count for much, Mr Treasurer; but I would point out that a Statute of the College,

70

which has never been rescinded, lays down that the Treasurer-ship may not be held along with a minor-canonry in the Cathedral.'

And behold it was so. The Treasurer found that he could not, by statute, hold a plurality of offices and had to drop his minor-canonry.

However, not even that triumph served to soothe the Professor's inferiority-complex, or whatever it was he suffered from. He continued to be as feeble and vacillating, in general, as before.

He even suffered from a mild form of agoraphobia: he could not walk openly across the cloister court as others did, or even diagonally over the lawn in the open: he had to keep to the wall of the cloisters themselves, with his back to the wall, as if for support.

The phrase describing the custom in medieval churches — 'the weak go to the wall' — was exemplified in him. His persecutor, the Treasurer, said that the Professor had formed the habit at school from having had his posterior kicked so often.

Someone more friendly than the bullying Treasurer met the Professor, one day towards the end, sidling along the cloisters, back to the wall as usual. When spoken to, all the poor fellow said was,

'I can't sleep, I can't sleep.'

That night he took an overdose of chloral, and was found death in his bed under the arch of the roof-beam.

At once the Treasurer claimed that set as next in seniority. True it was that none of the other vicars-choral fancied those rooms, at any rate so immediately after what had happened in them.

The Treasurer had no such qualms. A stout, rubicund bully of a man, he was quite insensitive to atmosphere, completely extrovert.

A bachelor, he had been successful at running the business affairs of the College and, at forty-five, could look forward to moving up to a fat prebend in the Cathedral, when one of them fell in. (A prebend seemed to operate as a preservative: the prebendaries were a lot of unconscionably aged dodderers — no retiring age in those days.)

The Treasurer's hobby was archaeology. He too was particularly interested in Walls. He had gone boldly into print with a theory of his on the 'Giant's Hedge' that runs across country between the River Fowey and the River Looe, cutting off, or protecting, a large cantle of the best land south of Bodmin Moor. The folklore rhyme ran:

> The Devil, having nothing else to do,
> Built a great hedge from Lerryn to Looe.

Recently the Treasurer had turned his attention to the Roman Wall and, with his business instincts, was making a special study of the coins turning up there.

Not a man to take much interest in the furnishing of his rooms — like so many Victorians he had no taste and had typically installed a bare brass bed with knobs under the fine black oak beam above — he yet took some pride in the quasi-archaeological details of the set.

The sitting room was equipped with a large Caroline chimney piece — black oak, heavily carved, heraldic shields with coats-of-arms, scrolls and finials, what not. The bedroom upstairs had retained its oak shutters, with the original iron hasps; the door had kept its ancient latch; the clothes-press in the wall sported decorative dolphin hinges, just as they had been fixed in those improving Laudian times on the threshold of disaster.

In quiet Victorian days grass grew in the deserted alleys in the old quarter below the cathedral — in summer vacation when Bishop and Dean, prebendaries and canons were mostly away; and even the College of Vicars-choral was closed during August.

On one of those delicious days, with not a soul about, the Treasurer came back from the Roman Wall, and quietly hanged himself from the convenient beam above his bed.

No one could think why. He had been a cheerful extrovert, a bullying kind of man with no nerves. There was no motive that anyone could think of — no worries, certainly no money troubles.

For a time there was a hoo-doo upon that desirable set above the cloisters. No one applied for those rooms.

*

When, after some time, a new-comer arrived — a stranger to those parts, who knew nothing about the macabre associations of those rooms — he was put into them, the best set in the College. As it happened, a young man, he was peculiarly sensitive to atmosphere and a bit invalidish, highly strung. (Unlike the Treasurer who had strung himself up on that beam.)

This young man, decidedly a junior, had never had a room of his own before and identified himself happily with the beautiful setting his career as a vicar-choral had acquired. There was the southward view across city and river to the distant hills. On the other side a glimpse of the cathedral, and the spire of St Philip and St James. The place echoed with the sound of bells, which he loved.

Then there was the sheer beauty of the rooms themselves, a withdrawn — sometimes, he fancied a wounded — beauty, as if waiting for something: a revelation? Within, he was much taken with the effects of light from there being windows on both sides: a honey-coloured bar lying athwart the room at sunset from the west, pale lemon lying on window-sill with the dawn; a ruddy glow from firelight upon dark oak.

73

In short, he fell in love with those rooms, felt them to be *his*, identified them with himself.

Revelation was not long in coming — a rude, a brutal awakening from his dream.

In the middle of a dreary November afternoon — it was All Souls day, full of shadows and ghosts — a thoughtless colleague, catching the newcomer at the foot of the staircase leading up to his rooms, told him their story.

He was thunderstruck, horrified — as if he had been dealt a blow. — As, in effect, he had been.

That night he had the greatest difficulty in going to sleep under that sinister beam for his imaginings. Many a night thereafter he awoke in a sweat of fear, heart beating out of his body.

Yet it never occurred to him to give up. It all added a further dimension, a more poignant feeling to his occupancy — as if he were himself involved in the story.

Actually there was little enough light that he could gather as to the previous occupants. No one would tell him anything about his predecessors, *why* they had done what they had, or probe into possible motives. After all, he was a newcomer — none of his business, nor was the colleague who had blurted out the facts in that irresponsible fashion at all highly regarded. After that episode, a conspiracy of silence settled around him; and, for his part, he never communicated to anyone what he endured there night after night.

A curious result was that, little as he had gleaned about the Professor and the Treasurer, he felt more intimately aware of them than the members of the College who had known them in the flesh. His colleagues, after all, were a normally imperceptive lot. They had no inkling as to why the Treasurer had followed the Professor — the persecutor and the persecuted — down the dusky corridor of death.

74

The newcomer thought that he had, from what little he gleaned about the two of them. He formed a theory, or the conception formed in his mind, after much brooding, that life somehow lost its savour for the Treasurer, after the death of the man whom it was his one pleasure to tease and torment. Chapman had always been there, a fixture in the scene: when he was no longer there, the stronger character sorely missed his presence, the weakness that could always elicit a response, a snub, an exposure. Some sense of purpose went out of the other's life with the disappearance of his opposite number, his familiar victim. There was a vacancy; polarity, balance, was lost.

At any rate, such was the young man's explanation, or construction. No one had any other. No one could explain the sequence: the two suicides seemed in no way connected.

The newcomer thought otherwise.

For himself, having worked it out for himself, he became gradually reconciled to the facts. The macabre facts no longer spoiled the enchantment of those rooms for him, but added pathos. In the ruddy winter firelight it was like looking into the heart of a rose.

The years passed over his head. When an offer of another set of rooms in College came his way subsequently, he had no difficulty in refusing it. Nor was it precisely — as the normally imperceptive thought — that it was because he had 'lived down' those memories that he refused to change and leave them behind; it was because of them that he chose to remain.

IX

The Paragon

'Who was the handsomest man you have known?' — The rather absurd question was put to a small circle of intimates who remained round the table at an ancient College, dinner over, dessert placed on the shining mahogany, candles lit, little pools of light reflected amid the coloured Crown Derby.

The older members of the party were all agreed upon Giles Madron. The one younger man present was not convinced — but, then, he had not known Madron in his heyday, the splendour and flourish, the others agreed, in his youth. He had come across him only on his visits as a guest to the College during the Second German War. Whereas his prime had been just before the First War.

Evidently one would have to dig and dig back into the past to get at the secret of this buried, this wasted life.

The younger Fellow, invalidish, hard-working, and regrettably serious-minded himself, had no use for Giles Madron. He regarded him as the cultivated waster he was, and used to refer to him as a 'clever silly' — this to a colleague of his own age who made rather a cult of persons of that type. The colleague was Madron's *protégé*, or perhaps Madron was his *protégé*, since he brought him as a guest to the College at which Madron had been expected to win a Fellowship.

Perhaps he had not taken it seriously. But he never took anything seriously: this was his foible, his pose, the stance he had taken up since any of them knew him — until it entered into the marrow of his being and made his life what it was.

What ever was the explanation of it? What made him *tick*?

No one knew.

He had a sly and sophisticated sense of humour, which expressed itself as often as not in Latin — for he was an exquisite classical scholar. He lived his life inside the inverted commas of irony — this gave him many laughs at the expense of other people and their absurdities. A further irony was that he did not know that his absurdities were being observed by the industrious researcher, whom he disregarded (as not being a classical scholar).

He would be brought as a guest for a week-end during the Second War, to the annoyance of the conscientious Bursar, for the guest would gaily consume the College rations, which were very restricted during that war. Madron was merely amused by the broad hints of the Bursar, who became a character in the fantasy-menagerie of fools he constructed (perhaps hardly appreciating that he was one of the greatest himself. Or perhaps he did? He was subtle enough for anything.)

It amused him that the cook of that august institution should have been heard to say obsequiously over the counter at Sainsbury's:

'Please can I have two pounds of sausage-meat for— College?'

When the dour Bursar — to restrict the consumption of coals in the Smoking Room grate — took away the diminutive poker, the unwanted guest was delighted and got his young friend to procure that instrument to show round as a trophy in his London clubs.

When the war was over, and the Bursar retired, Madron presented the College with a silver snuff-box with a pointed Latin inscription:

'Grato *tamen* animo' (i.e. with a grateful mind *nevertheless*).

During the war, when asked what he was doing, he would put finger to lip as if to suggest something hush-hush. Simple folk concluded — he was laughing at them as usual — that he was doing secret war-work of importance. He was, of course, doing nothing.

*

Unknown to the ironist's young friend — and it might have disturbed even the ironist himself, if he could have known it — the simple-minded researcher they both rather discounted was quietly doing a little research into Giles Madron's earlier life. Serious-minded, incurably inquisitive, bent on fulfilling his vocation, he was genuinely puzzled at what made so clever a man so silly. Why was he *bent* on wasting his talents, throwing away a life which had begun with such promise?

He discovered that at school he had been known as 'the Paragon'. For of the seventy boys in College he was not only the cleverest and handsomest, but hardly less good at games — Captain of Boats and, in his last year, Captain of School. That was indeed his apogee.

In that year too he attracted the attention of the Provost — bearer of a famous name — of the College at Cambridge where he had won a scholarship. Perhaps 'won' was hardly the word for it: no hard labour was involved, it was expected that he would step into it, and he slipped into it easily, as he slipped into everything.

What he 'won' was the ardent affection of the celebrated, and celibate, Provost who had never tasted quite such exquisite nectar before. He confided to his diary, his chief confidant: 'I have never known such love as that I feel for young Giles Madron — brilliantly gifted, tall and very handsome, with a slight outward look of the eye which is all the more disturbing. Is he focusing upon one, or is he not? He is exquisitely sensitive, and it seems that he is responsive. He is extraordinarily intuitive, but how far does the response go? I cannot believe that I can be so fortunate as to win his love, with the years between us, and unattractive as I must be to such a paragon. We shall see. Meanwhile, he gives me such happiness as I have not known, contingent as it is.'

To the Provost, an apprehensive soul, everything was contingent, and much of his conversation was in the elaborate conditional. But within the cosy outward cocoon was wrapped a simple nature; though a generation older, his heart was still that of a boy, of Giles's age. A celebrated, and rather alarming, scholar to the world outside, he longed in a rather lonely exalted life for intimacy and companionship.

This at last he achieved with Giles, who responded to his interests and had, at this time, a somewhat similar nature. Even apart from scholarship and literature, where the youth was quite precocious, they enjoyed their games together — word-games, card-games, and a peculiar fetish of the Provost's.

This was not the boot-fetish of a well-known friend of his, who would manoeuvre his young friends into treading upon him, under the guise of religious humility. The Provost's devotions, though not himself a religious believer, were utterly, perhaps disappointingly, Platonic.

But his fetish was hardly less original.

As the two went about the country on holiday together they made a habit of secreting a *cache* of coins in a cairn or outcrop of rock; finding a hole in a Cornish carn — made either by the weather or exploratory miners — into which to stuff their coppers for some future generation to discover. No hoax, just a schoolboy game — but what was the Freudian significance of it?

Young Giles would come to stay at the Provost's agreeable house in the country — his hide-out from College business, which in truth he detested. He rather hated being Provost; but, as a kind colleague said, he would have hated *not* being Provost more. So, there were the chores; at his place in the country were his consolations.

Above all, at this time, Giles.

Their literary games were no less enjoyable: Giles could, amazingly, keep up with the Provost. In Greek, for example, for which Giles had a special gift. One day the Provost came out with the lines from Shakespeare's Sonnets, for which they had a shared cult:

> Shall I compare thee to a summer's day?
> Thou art more lovely and more temperate.

Straight away, without a moment's hesitation, Giles responded with a translation into Greek hexameters.

But how far did he respond in other ways?

One autumn evening, before the university term began with its boredoms and its bores, they were together before the hospitable fire in the library at Great Minford, Giles lounging on the hearthrug beside the Provost's deep armchair, when the fine head of auburn hair settled itself comfortably against the Provost's knee. The Provost was in bliss — a mark of such favour from someone half his age! A mark of confidence. But *was* it confidence? Could it last?

The elderly scholar's characteristic self-questioning set itself in train: it was a contingent bliss. It could not be expected to last. Everything in life was uncertain for him, contingent.

That winter term the contingency arose.

He received a letter from Giles to tell him that he had fallen for someone of his own age, one Cecil Astbury, youngest member of a foremost political family. Indeed, his father was leader of a political party at that time threatening to split. There were many deserters, described by opponents as rats deserting the sinking ship.

Young Cecil was already known for his quip: 'What were the rats supposed to do? — line up on the bridge with the Captain?'

It was Cecil's wit as much as his disenchanted view of things that seduced Giles and drew him away.

The Paragon

The Provost could not but be envious — and yet it was no more than he had expected all along.

*

Shortly, in 1914, the greater contingency of the war arose, which took both young men away to the Front, from which Cecil did not return.

Giles, fortunate as ever, surprisingly came through unscathed, unharmed. He won no medals, but somehow he survived, when most of those with whom he had been at school had fallen.

Was he in fact unharmed? Though not even once wounded, had received no physical damage — looks unchanged, except that he had broadened out into manhood — had there not been some secret wound to the spirit?

It was another of the puzzles that stimulated the simple mind of the researcher, straightforward, uncomplicated, but incisive as a surgeon's knife.

For Giles emerged a strange, inexplicable man.

He was expected to compete for the prize Fellowship at the College of which, later, he came to make such fun. At that time, this was the 'blue ribbon' of the university, and it was a surprise when Giles Madron, of all people, did not make the grade.

Perhaps he could not be bothered to try very hard: he came to make a point — was it a point of pride? — of not trying very hard at anything.

And shortly he had no need to. For again, to people's surprise, he married; when hitherto he had shown not the slightest interest in the opposite sex. It was a rich woman whom he married, who adored him. After that, he needed to do nothing, and proceeded to do nothing discernible for the rest of his life.

He was fond enough of the wife who provided for his

wants, in his detached, inscrutable manner. But was the marriage ever consummated?

That the industrious observer could never find out.

There were no children to distract him from doing nothing. Her family urged her to leave him. But he could always have whistled her back, for she loved him, and she had got him.

*

He certainly had an odd, engaging turn of humour.

One day he gave lunch to a contemporary who *had* achieved the Fellowship he had missed at the College he rather fancied in his inconsequent, teasing way. Together they consumed a bottle of Grande Chartreuse. Emerging into the Park, the contemporary said, 'We must be careful.'

Half-way across the Park both felt the need to relieve nature, and looked for a Public Convenience. When they eventually found one, it was locked, with a notice to indicate that it would be opening in May. They could not wait till May and, scouting round, found the attendant, who said that those were the orders from above.

'Who gave the orders?' said Madron.

'The First Commissioner of Works,' said the attendant.

'This *is* the First Commissioner of Works,' said Madron solemnly, pointing to his companion.

The door was unlocked, and they were ushered in respectfully, deferentially.

*

What was it that made him tick?

Had something been killed in him by his experience of war when so young, that he could never take human beings seriously again? He seemed to be perpetually playing a game with them, in which he was very fly and self-aware, never caught out.

He had a succession of bogus jobs in the City that occupied some part of some days. He was a member of a dozen clubs, though 'I never confess to more than seven.' He confided to his young friend that he 'found it useful to have one club on either side of the road, in case one came out a little confused after dinner.' Hence both Brooks's *and* White's.

In the afternoon he would do the round of the second-hand bookshops and the antique-shops which were the joy of London in those days, to the like-minded. He collected rare books and silver — and had a very choice, not large, collection of each.

It was over book-collecting — no greater bond — that he made the acquaintance of his young friend of similar background, scholarship, and tastes.

This elect young man, another item in the collection, would receive a formally phrased invitation, 'Pray, do me the honour', etc. There would follow a very well chosen dinner at Brooks's. Or, occasionally: 'My wife is deserting me for the Opera. Would you make one of a small company to console me?' A hand-picked few would enjoy a choice dinner at his home (if such it could be called). At 11 p.m. she would appear at the door, blow him a kiss and up to bed on her own. (Each of them fastidious, they had separate bedrooms. They lived most of their lives separately.)

*

At last the younger friend, having made the grade, graduated to dine alone with the couple. They lived in plain luxury, tastes simple but expensive. Everything appointed of the best, furniture, rugs, delicious French clocks on chimney-pieces; the service itself like clockwork.

It was evident that he was *bored*.

This had begun on their honeymoon (if that was the word for it). An addict of music, she had insisted on taking him to the Opera at Salzburg — and he couldn't bear music. There was one thing he felt strongly about. He made her come out after the second act. Never again.

After that she went regularly to concerts or the Opera, usually on her own, leaving him to his own devices, or to entertain himself with his men friends. He could not be better pleased.

She loved him; he remained always good-looking; he gave her no cause for suspicion — there were no other women; she had him to herself. Or so she thought.

Suddenly, without a word of warning, he snapped and died. She was heart-broken.

*

Then she began to go through his things, his books and papers. He had a fine collection of Dr Johnson, original first editions, some with marginalia. It was sold for a good sum to America, dollars much in demand just then.

He had a taste for inscriptions, usually obscure jokes in Latin, variations on A.D., Anno Domini, for example. A.S.H., which one sometimes sees on 18th century monuments: *Anno Salutis Humanae*, was denominated The Dodo.

He had collected a Book of Sayings, which he had never got round to publishing. He had been fond of giving utterance to such sayings himself — as, during the Second War: 'I am the civilisation they are fighting for' — which, in a way, he was.

What to make of it all? What kind of a man had he been?

Lovingly, with increasing curiosity, she went through his papers. At the bank were his diaries — or, rather, engagement books, calendars — for he had been too lazy to keep diaries.

*

At this point she was electrified. She discovered that he had kept a flat in another part of London. Whatever for?

Evidently for assignations.

Here was a life she had known nothing about. She began to be frantically jealous — posthumously, uselessly, all the more insatiably.

She found out that he had had two women friends. One of them was a not very successful highbrow actress, to whom he gave fur-coats — out of *her* money. There were entries in the calendars of visits at the flat, but never the name of the actress — the entry took the form of tea with a friend.

Now frantic with curiosity and jealousy, she set on foot inquiries — and found, paradoxically to her disappointment, that this had been a purely intellectual affair. This hurt her, curiously, more than if it had been a passionate love-affair, a normal affair of the heart. It was more wounding, for it revealed to her how *bored* he had been, how boring he had found life with her.

Pursuing her inquiries further she found that there had been a second woman. This was still more maddening, for it was the wife of a foremost political figure of those days, a beautiful woman, rather bored by her self-absorbed husband, a tremendous egoist bent on fame.

It appeared that Madron's meeting with her had formed the one romantic episode of his life. The handsome young officer, returned from the War, had gone up to the carriage of this subsequently famous woman, presented himself, and was graciously received. Becoming friends, they too used to meet for tea and talk at the flat.

Or, perhaps, Tea and Sympathy, for it seemed that nothing else happened at the snug little bachelor flat, hemmed in by rows of books. For he did read, and their talk was mainly of literature.

Whatever their talk was about, Bettina — such was the name of the Lady — must ultimately have grown bored with its leading to no point, nothing, as was the way with this clever, disenchanted man. She became rather disabused herself, and the strange affair − if 'affair' it could be called − petered out. Like everything with him.

How mysterious a man, she thought − this had intrigued her at the beginning, her own famous husband all too rhetorically obvious. But she never penetrated any further into the mystery, and gave him up. Or somehow it just lapsed.

*

But what were the mysterious figures his widow noticed written down in the calendars about the time of his friendship with the second Egeria? Were they the minutes the assignation lasted? Were they the duration of——?

She grew hysterical − frustrated love, curiosity, jealousy for the passion she had never been able to excite.

Humiliated, she consulted the young friend who had known her husband better than she had done herself. He brought in the Industrious Observer over the riddle − who had solved the problem of Shakespeare's Sonnets, to everyone's annoyance.

Together, putting two and two together in the simplest possible fashion − the royal road to success − they solved the riddle for her.

What had been Giles's most prized possession?

He had possessed the most perfect gold watch in the world, a gift of hers, of which he was exceedingly proud. Every year he used to take it to Switzerland to have it kept in perfect condition.

These figures were the seconds by which it was fractionally out.

His widow was not at all grateful to have the mystery solved − any more than Shakespeare 'scholars' were to have the problem of the Sonnets worked out for them.

It made her feel more inadequate than ever (as the other made *them*). The emptiness, the strangeness, of his life stood revealed. All her own life she had been married to a stranger; nor did she know him, she felt, any better now. Worst of all, it brought home to her that she herself had been found wanting.

X

The Conceited Scholar

The eminent scholar was very conceited. And, after all —
come to think of it — was he really eminent?

He had had first-class classical training at a famous Public
School which specialised in it; then he had gone up to Cambridge, where he got no better than a Second in the Classical
Tripos. This, in a way, marked him for life; it gave him a
complex, an inferiority-complex which expressed itself in a
vein of superciliousness. He believed himself, however, to be
superior. Perhaps he was. He was a good Grecian, after the
manner of the great Jebb.

He need not have nourished such a scunner against life,
for he made up for his Second with a brilliant thesis which
won him, in the Cambridge manner, a Fellowship at his
College.

This he retained all his life as a bachelor — at least, technically a bachelor.

But, restless and unsatisfied, he departed from the groves
of Academe for the Civil Service. There, taken abroad by a
Cabinet Minister who happened to be a Labour man, a
Trade Unionist, young Mr Bice diverted himself by circulat-
ing squibs satirising his Minister's style of speech, his gram-
matical errors, dropped aiches, etc.

He invented the story of the Minister, who was on friendly
terms with the King, addressing him with:

'Your Majesty, I've such an 'orrible 'eadache.'

'Take a couple of aspirates, Mr Bice.'

Quite untrue, of course, for King George V was as

innocent of knowing what is an aspirate as the Minister himself.

The Minister, however, knew two to that clever young man's one, and got him promptly de-railed.

His Civil Service prospects ended, he got a posting in the International Bank in Vienna (the later failure of which started the train of events leading to the World Depression). He, however, had failed some time before that: he had no eye or ear for economics, let alone finance.

On leave from Austria, he went down into the country for the weekend with a learned lady of his acquaintance — and never came away again.

She had plenty of means of her own, quite enough for two. They had scholarly interests in common. They never married — much too high-minded for that. He never needed to have a job again. Now he could go back to his scholarship, prove himself, make his name at last.

In fact, he moved on. He did not go back to the waste land of Greek grammar; he moved forward into the fertile border-lands of English history and literature, carrying his standards of classical scholarship with him. There he had a distinct advantage — and he *did* make a name at last for himself.

He was aided in this as he grew older by a small circle of young men from his own famous School, who made a cult of him. They addressed him as Master, deferred to him — and even referred to him outside the circle — as 'the Master'.

They were laughing at him, of course; it was one of the many games they played in that circle. He had no idea of it; he fell for it completely. It rather turned his head. But he did resume his scholarly interests, and took to writing. His books were short, mostly bits and pieces. The circle, however, loyally puffed them — part of their regard for him was sincere — and his reputation rose in consequence.

An outsider at his College, an outsider to the circle and their School — indeed of any Public School — whom *they* regarded with no friendly eye, had his reservations. He would sometimes put the question — what did the bits and pieces *add up to*?

Since their own bits and pieces did not add up to much, they did not much like the question. Nor did they like the questioner: they united to depreciate him and his work. He survived and — since he had more justice of mind than they had — he allowed that J. M. Bice (who was now celebrated enough to be known by his initials alone, as 'J.M.', 'the great J.M.', or 'the Master') was a very clever man and extremely interesting to talk to.

*

And so his hostess, or whatever she was to him, found.

He was not physically attractive; but, then, neither was she. The attraction was intellectual.

On the other hand, he was a good figure of a man, tall and broad, with large bluish hands, singularly inept, as he was physically clumsy. A heterosexual characteristic — and he was entirely hetero, in so far as he had any interest in sex.

His nose was the only indication: large and fleshy, pointed and, even so, slightly *retroussé*, it was, like the Younger Pitt's, 'turned up at all the world'. It had a singular habit of twitching on its own, as if detecting a nasty smell in the Combination Room, whenever he returned there. The outsider — more observant than the circle gave him credit for, or indeed than they were themselves — was much amused by this nervous *tic*: he regarded it as a sexual symptom, as perhaps it was.

Only once did the great J.M. give himself away. He was speaking about good Queen Victoria, in whom he had an almost proprietary interest and spoke of her with such familiarity as if he were a privileged member of her entourage. He suddenly let drop a phrase about the Prince Consort's 'wearily grinding out the chore of marital duty.'

In a flash the outsider saw into the circumstances of the other man's extra-marital life, which he shared with the Etruscan scholar at her house in the country, where she maintained him: in effect, kept him.

*

It was an interesting establishment that they had at Qu'acre — short for Queen's Acre (the circle naughtily referred to it, guying J.M.'s antiquarian interests, as Ye Olde Cow-Byre). And, of course, it was dominated — and so was J.M. — by its owner, the formidable Miss Monica Straight.

The buildings indeed looked like an old cow-byre, which part of them may well have been. For, curiously, the house consisted of the outbuildings of a large country-house which had been there but had long been pulled down.

Qu'acre consisted of the big former kitchen, dairy, scullery, larders, cider-house, bakery, what not — the dependencies of the great house, arranged around an inner court-yard: now transformed. It made an utterly fascinating place: old doors with hasps and clattering latches, shutters, big beams and rafters, cubby-holes — you never knew what antiquarian junk you might find in them, flints, arrow-heads, spindle-whorls, *fibulae*; holes and corners crammed with books.

It was a very bookish house, with the joint interests of J.M. and Monica, books continually arriving, constantly overflowing. There was, in fact, a large library: a big square room with a too low ceiling rather on top of you. But that made it cosy and comfortable out there in the woldy country of the Cambridgeshire-Suffolk border when the winter winds swept across.

*

In spite of the Old Cow-Byre's allure, the circle did not make much use of it, or respond to its not over-pressing invitations.

91

The truth was that they did not care for Miss Monica Straight.

She was too mannish a woman for them — the fact that she was a woman at all was against her in that exclusively masculine admiration society which the circle constituted. They preferred to see J.M. at his or their London clubs, or during his visits to College.

If one of them went down to Qu'acre, he found the conversation dominated by Monica. The Master was not particularly talkative; he preferred to be oracular, saving himself up to interpose with the *mot juste*, a conclusive phrase or quoted epigram. He had a marvellous memory, and a vast fund of quotations. Sententiously, he gave judgement.

But not so much in her presence. She ruled the roost. Not only that, but — what was objectionable to the circle, brought up in the traditions of ancient houses and colleges — when dinner was over and dessert and port appeared, she did not withdraw but remained on and on drinking port and holding forth. It was impossible to have any intimate talk or fun with the Master in her presence.

And then — to fill up the cup of wrath against her — she would smoke her pipe!

None of the circle smoked a pipe; rather delicately, in a finicking kind of way, they would smoke a cigarette. One of them went so far as to favour a cigar, with much fuss and fume, and dallying over the ritual.

This was the favourite who ultimately emerged as Provost of the College, very properly, as against the outsider. He had all the votes of their old School, about a third of the total for a start — including of course that of J.M. So he was under an obligation, and recognised it.

But he could not abide a woman smoking a pipe (or woman as such, come to that).

Monica Straight got no credit for being half a man. She had a large mannish figure, dressed very tweedily, and even in those distant days was often to be seen about the place in a pair of slacks, a man's woollen jersey over little in the way of mamillary development.

However, she provided a firm framework for J.M.'s life — without her, he was singularly helpless. He always had been clumsy with his hands and had no practical aptitudes whatever.

*

Then she fell ill, and was a helpless invalid lingering for some time before she died.

How he managed during that period the outside observer never learned. But what J.M.'s attitude was may be partially glimpsed from a dream he had — and, oddly enough, wrote out for him in his distinguished hand, that of a scholar, self-conscious and elegant. Here it is for what a psychologist, Freudian or otherwise, may make of it.

I wanted to get away from the house I had been in and was running down a straight road away from it, when I saw a cloud or column of snow approaching on the right, as high as a house. Soundlessly the snow thickened, coming towards me like an advancing wall, not rising from the ground but coming from the sky. I made up my mind to rush through it, though there was a danger of getting drowned in snow.

I had thought of making a sort of shelter for myself at the end of the wall or against a tree, when it cleared up, and I came out on to a length of road free from snow. I began running in lazy curves from side to side — as one makes curves with a bicycle going uphill to ease the gradient — leaning inwards like a skater as I made each curve. (This was an old trick of mine when running in real life, and it gave me pleasure to do it in my dream.)

I crossed a high road, thinking that I was now nearing my destination. Running down a slope away from it, I encountered several people — there was an atmosphere of confusion: evidently there had been an accident.

At this moment I saw beside me in the road what I immediately recognised as the trunk of a woman, with no head or limbs — a sort of bundle, clean cut at the ends, no blood — rolling down the hill. I broke into a walk in order not to seem to be running away-from it, but I had to walk very quickly to get away from it. I decided to get away from it and not to offer any help — partly because it disgusted me, and partly (but this was, I think, conscious self-justification) because I felt that there was nothing that I could do. I quickened my pace, looking straight in front of me, but I felt this thing rolling after me, so I had to walk still more rapidly for fear of being overtaken by it.

*

When Monica eventually died she left him the whole of the family fortune that had come to her — a tidy £25,000 or so. Quite enough to provide for him and see him through.

But what was he to do with the fag-end of his life, helpless and already afflicted with lameness down his right side, from a slight stroke? He now walked with a decided limp, or rather a dragging of one foot, with the aid of a hefty walking stick.

The Provost, his former favourite, invited the old man back into College, where he was a great nuisance from his physical incapacity, his querulousness, and utter helplessness. He practically needed a man-servant all to himself — and staff was short.

As his incapacity increased, he gave way to an appalling state of self-pity, sending for the Provost at all hours of the day to whine over his case. The Provost was not a particularly busy man, but he had no time to spare on these confessional *tête-à-têtes*. Former kindness gave way to complaints on both sides: words of candour − unspoken hitherto in the circle − and old scores came to the surface. The Provost ceased to be the favourite he had been; there was even a breach.

J.M. was ready to consider leaving College for good. The place was inconvenient for an invalid − draughty corridors, damp staircases in those days; sanitary conveniences, such as they were, not handy.

*

At this juncture there came to see the Provost, who invited him to stop the night at the Lodge, Monica's brother. He was a failed politician, a smooth customer who could exert professional charm, plausible, but somehow unconvincing.

He had had his moment, in the dreadful Thirties, as a notable proponent of Appeasement, a voluble and plausible supporter of the insupportable Chamberlain. There had been many of those in the unspeakable House of which he was a Member; but somehow he was memorable for the moralistic tone he conferred, the ethicality he gave to quite unethical propositions. In short, he was a humbug.

Now he was one of those who had been swept away by the political earthquake of 1945. He was both hard up *and* mean. He had been quietly furious when his sister had left all her money out of the family (she had detested *him*, and was determined that it should not come to him).

This was the politician's language he addressed to the Provost at the breakfast table. Helping himself to more than his share of bacon and eggs, he held forth:

'My wife and I feel that we owe an obligation to J.M., who was so devoted to my sister. And we realise what a problem he is in College. We have a spare floor in our house where we could put him up and look after him. We have some paying guests, but while getting ready and making arrangements with them to vacate, J.M. could go to a guest-house we know very well and can most strongly recommend.'

After a pause, he added: 'Of course, there would have to be testamentary arrangements. We could not afford it otherwise.'

Helping himself largely to marmalade, he said: 'In fact, in view of J.M.'s physical incapacity, we should have to have power of attorney.'

A shudder passed over the Provost as he realised what this meant: the old man helpless in the hands of this calculating couple.

He fixed his eyes, to steady himself and deflect scrutiny, on the disappearing marmalade.

*

However, College was a raw place in winter, without comforts. J.M. was not unwilling to consider a change, but made the usual fuss.

'How am I to get there?'
'By train.'
'How am I to get to the train?'
'By taxi.'
'How about the other end?'
'Monica's brother will meet you at the station and conduct you.'

*

He went.

Within forty-eight hours he was back − on his own steam. He had ordered a car to take him right back to College, a matter of forty miles. He would never specify the horror he had endured there. But the squalor must have been appalling, for he came back infested with vermin: he had to be deloused, de-fleaed and fumigated. He was quite sure that *they* would have poisoned him.

What the failed politician's precise intentions were one could not be sure. Was this to have been preliminary to better treatment, softening him up for those new testamentary dispositions in a grateful mood?

Or perhaps not?

XI

Mad Miss Moll

Do you know Arvethro? Though I have lived in Cornwall all my life I had never set eyes on it myself till only the other day. Never did house make a stranger, a more haunting impression on me, with its air of desertedness as if for ever waiting.

I first caught sight of it as I came round the bend of the road, as if waiting for *me*, in black December light, filtered through the trees. You can usually tell what was once a place of the old gentry — the road suddenly became an avenue of diminutive beeches, bitten off and flattened by the sea-winds; beneath the raised bank of the road were a couple of cottages, evidently those of dependents; and then the house itself, sombre, darkened by trees. What surprised me was its colour: it had a dark blood-red flush upon it, where Cornish houses are usually grey or green.

At the side was a derelict farm-yard entrance — nowadays no bustle of farming going ahead. I entered, treading the soft humus under foot: a copse of stunted beeches and oaks, then a long range of stable buildings, the roof in decay, large slates laid cross-wise. Ruin was given an air of distinction by a shapely cupola of the time of Queen Anne.

The path curved round to the front, a red sandstone façade, immense character given to it by an overlarge pediment with a venetian window beneath.

The shutters were shut. . . . Was there any sign of life, or of occupation? I looked up at the blank face of the house. Upstairs the shutters were not drawn in the tall middle

98

window, faded curtains looped in an old fashioned way that gave it a Victorian look; between them a dingy white looking-glass.

I rang the bell, half fearing that some crazed old lunatic would appear.

The bell rang in the empty hall inside; but no one answered it.

I looked round. In front of the house was bare rock; what had been the lawn had gone to grass, with overhanging ilexes shadowing the house, the brambles encroaching on either side. The enclosure was fenced off by a ha-ha. The field outside had been a tiny park; the drive had long been grown over; dwarf plantations to left and right.

And then there was the view. I suddenly saw with what sense of propriety the eighteenth century had chosen: everything was in perfect proportion, the house, the plantations, the little park, to the tiny bay which from here completed the landscape. There in the middle distance must be Carrick-howel: the rock beautifully shaped like a boat, with the steel-green sea boiling up round it and then pouring snow-white all over it.

Still no sign of life in the house, I skirted gingerly round. The wall of the garden bulged dangerously outwards; beyond it an unkempt wilderness that had been an orchard. There were old fruit-trees, but dying; ilexes and overgrown bushes of euonymus, and everywhere a sweet aromatic odour — whatever could it be? The house was almost impossible to approach here for rank vegetation. Crawling underneath the brambles I saw that a badgers' earth was established in the midst of what had been the fruit-garden.

From here one could see the devastation of the back wing, part of the roof had given in, part of the wall given out, the stones shuffled out like a pack of cards.

Never have I felt such a sense of desertion in a place, of desertion and, coupled with the air of distinction that yet peered through the ruin, of frustration. And all accentuated by the sweet, musky odour that arose from the winter heliotropes that flower in Cornwall in December and had covered the walled garden with their thick carpet.

Such was Arvethro. It was not until I had left it that the moon rose; and what with the curious lie of the bay and the roads all running away from it, it seemed to me that the moon was in the west. 'But surely the moon does not rise in the west?' I remember thinking before sleep overwhelmed me. Perhaps it was my head that was turned.

*

Arvethro belonged during the last two centuries to a family of lesser Cornish gentry. On inheriting a larger place in the west, they sold it in Victorian times to a yeoman farmer on the way up. His name was William Henry Treviades — pronounced, by the way, Trevizzes: a good Cornish farming name, impossible to confuse with those of the gentry.

He had an only daughter, Mary Jane, for whom he, the mother being dead, was ambitious. She was the apple of his eye.

Without being pretty, she had a wistful attractiveness; pleasant regular features, well-turned lips, if a trifle pale. Unlike her father, who had too much blood in his head, she had very little colour; and her hair was so fair that, though tinged with gold in her younger years, it gave the impression of being ash-grey — which in time it became.

An air of refinement hung about her, of which her father was proud, though she was not really educated. What means were there for a girl in her position at that time to be so? She read a good deal on her own, especially poetry; and of the poets Mrs Hemans and Elizabeth Barrett Browning, and Mr Tennyson — rather in that order. Her father was proud enough of her interest in reading, for which he had had no time in a hard and pushful life.

He wanted her to become a lady. But whom was she to marry? He was not willing for her to marry anyone of his own station in life. She was not to be a farmer's wife. But who else was there in that neighbourhood?

Improbably enough, a candidate turned up: a quiet gentlemanly man, with some means of his own, small but unencumbered. He was something of a scholar − he had been to the university: he might have made a clergyman.

They read together − to her father's approval and satisfaction. After all, what did it matter if the young man's means were small? He was not so young either: a man old enough to know his own mind. Mary Jane would have the house and estate − really no more than a large farm, with a little house-property − after her father's death. With that they should be able to present a good face to the world.

There supervened the agricultural depression of the late seventies and eighties, which left William Henry with a holding into which he had sunk all his capital and which was now worth only one-third of what he had given for it. In the midst of his difficulties, with no sign of the position improving, he died, leaving his daughter and her undeclared suitor unmarried.

Perhaps it was that he was not a marrying sort? This possibility had not entered the direct and unambivalent mind of William Henry: to his mind his daughter was a good match, and her attached young man eligible. What, then, could be more natural, or indeed inevitable?

It is the way of some people to avoid the inevitable; and Arthur was one such.

To her his name appealed to something in the world of fantasy in which she lived, though she loved the name also for its bearer's sake. Her own name neither of them liked: they found it too plain and homely. They found a better in Mr Tennyson's poems − Mariana, which was just right, Arthur pointed out, being a romantic version of Mary Jane.

For her Arthur possessed the attraction of his intelligence, and his refinement. He painted a bit, he rode a bit, he even wrote a bit, and he read a great deal — though not, it would seem, to much purpose. The fact was that he was no hand at making a living. He recognised that: how could he therefore ever marry? he put it to himself.

Meanwhile, there was the bother of her father's affairs, the entanglements left to her. Arthur had no business head and no liking for farming: here he was no use to her.

One way in which his influence took effect: Mary Jane now went to church. She had been brought up a Methodist: another barrier between her and the neighbouring gentry, for who ever heard of a Methodist landed gentry? They went to church together. But not in the sense of the poet:

> Oh, peal upon our wedding,
>   And we will hear the chime,
> And come to church in time.[1]

*

Some years went by in this state, the affair between them never advancing or receding, though they were much alone together. They read and walked and talked; they drew and sketched all over the place. They filled albums with views of the headland, the cliffs, the bay, Carrickhowel. Or while Arthur read she embroidered. The farm-bailiff rendered what accounts he chose and didn't cheat her too much: the Cornish have a nice feeling for what is 'fitty' in these matters.

One day while they were sitting out on the lawn under the ilexes in summer, reading 'The Coming of Arthur' — the blue bay gleaming through the trees, the coast glimmering in the haze towards Tintagel — Arthur came to the passage:

> For saving I be joined
> To her that is the fairest under heaven,

[1] *A Shropshire Lad*, A. E. Housman.

I seem as nothing in the mighty world
And cannot will my will, nor work my work
Wholly, nor make myself in mine own realm
Victor and lord. But were I joined with her,
Then might we live together as one life,
And reigning with one will in everything
Have power on this dark land to lighten it,
And power on this dead world to make it live.

Looking up, he caught a look in her eyes, a question; was it a reproach? Instinctively, hardly consciously, he turned what might have become emotion into the safer channels of reflection and instruction.

Sometimes they went about visiting the places that came into the poems, especially Tintagel, which they saw not as a ruin, so much mumbled rubble, but as the poet saw it

> half in sea, and high on land,
> A crown of towers;

or they fancied they saw Isolt the Queen sitting at her casement

> A low sea-sunset glorying round her hair;

or Tristram meeting the 'lone woman weeping near a cross', and they wondered which of the way-side crosses near Tintagel that would be. Once they made an excursion to Dozmary, thinking of it as the pool into which Sir Bedivere cast Excalibur.

They made a curious couple going about those cliffs and moors; but there were few enough people to see them, and there was never anyone with them.

The first singularity that declared itself in Mary Jane's behaviour was during Arthur's absence, when she ceased to go to church; or went at odd times to moon about by herself, instead of going to service of a Sunday. This was not lost upon the parish.

When Arthur returned, Mary Jane proposed in a spurt of animation that they should go to the parish-feast the following week.

Together they went to the fair, where all the natural vivacity of Cornish people came to the surface. There were booths and standings, tents with trestle-tables with trays of limpets and mussels and shrimps. Arthur remembered having read that one of the cottages at Arvethro had been held by the service of a pie made of limpets, raisins and herbs, rendered on the eve of the feast-day. In the afternoon, sports; in the evening paraffin flares were lit, the roundabout started up and all the parish flocked in to make merry.

The evening was of a disturbing beauty. The moon had risen early, and already the bay was filled with an unearthly radiance, the light of another world, remote and strange. Carrickhowel gleamed in the middle distance, rimmed with silver.

The eeriness of the evening had an effect on his companion, or was it that the excitement of the fair had turned her head? She certainly talked strangely on the way home, at times incoherently.

Arthur was anxious to get her home as soon as possible to Arvethro. She loitered on the way, looking out on the rare spectacle the bay made. It seemed as if the whole moonlit sea were marching past. When he suggested moving on, she stopped to say:

> The house of Arvethro
> Belonged to King Jethro.

And then, looking out to the island:

> And Carrickhowel
> To the tribe of the owl.

He could get no sense out of her. It seemed from what she was saying that she thought that Carrickhowel had put a spell on the house. She went rambling on about the old story of the people hereabouts — of the man who had been sentenced to die, and cast out upon that rock with a pitcher of water and a loaf of bread into the setting sun.

As they came round the bend of the road, two or three children, excited by the fair, waited for the couple to pass and then one of them quite distinctly called after them,

'Mad Miss Moll! There goes Mad Miss Moll.'

So that was it! The village children took for granted what he had not even suspected.

Her crisis over, and the energy drained out of her with her chatter, it was a forlorn pair that entered in at the gate, went slowly up the drive, one on each side of the road. At the top they passed into the sombre cavern of the ilexes. The moonlight wavered through the feathery plumes of the trees upon the cold, withdrawn front of the house.

At the door she turned, supporting herself a little, held out a hand to him and with crazy dignity, said good-bye. She rang the bell, which clamoured cavernously inside the house; the door opened and she went in.

*

Was this then the end of their long courtship, this the end to which it had all been leading?

Arthur had been given his *congé*, which was also his excuse, his alibi. What was he to do?

He drifted noiselessly from place to place, making no disturbance, no displacement. From time to time he took a post, a tutorship, or taught school. The years consumed him.

For her, life became ever lonelier. She did not go to church at all now. Sometimes she wandered in the evenings, especially at sunset, and roamed the headland, looking out long and questioningly towards Carrickhowel.

As she faded she developed the curious charm of the 'touched', as we say. She had a great tenderness for children, and had a swing made for them among the fruit-trees in the walled garden, hoping they might come, though never a one came. Sometimes she fancied that one of them was tip-toeing behind her, saying, 'There goes Mad Miss Moll.' She watched the droves of little birds that fled before the wind and sheltered in the trees about the house. Yet sometimes she heard them too say: 'Miss Moll! Miss Moll! Mad, mad!'

Then she would take refuge upstairs in her room by the looking-glass, where in the years before she used to fancy herself the Lady of Shalott and look out for Arthur coming up the drive. Or she was Mariana, no longer just poor mad Miss Moll, but Mariana in the Moated Grange:

> And ever when the moon was low,
>   And the shrill winds were up and away,
> In the white curtain, to and fro,
>   She saw the gusty shadow sway.
> But when the moon was very low,
>   And wild winds bound within their cell,
>   The shadow of the ilex fell
> Upon her bed, across her brow.
> She only said, 'The night is dreary,
>   He cometh not', she said;
> She said, 'I am aweary, aweary,
>   I would that I were dead'.

In the end, she fell ill. Word of it reached Arthur and he set out to come. She had the sense that he was coming at last: this rallied her and threw her into a happy agitation. As she felt him approaching, already evening, she dressed herself in bridal attire. Leaving the hall-door open for him, she went up to her accustomed place at the window to watch and wait. The moon was rising through the ilexes and already a path of silver lay across the bay towards Carrickhowel. The ilexes suddenly gave a shudder, as if a light went out.

A shadow crossed the drive. Arthur went up to the door and rang timidly. No answer.

He rang a second time: the bell clanged through the house, he thought, fit to wake the dead.

Upstairs in front of the looking-glass, book in hand open at 'The Coming of Arthur', head fallen forward, she seemed, in the moonlight, asleep.

XII

St Carroc's Crucifix

St Carroc's was a most inaccessible place. How well I had reason to think so, I thought, when I paid my first visit to the young man taking possession. I had received an alarming paper of instructions how to get there. I was to make for St Greep church on the other side of the river Fowey. Now the Other Side of the River Fowey is a no-man's-land, where anything may happen. Beguilingly beautiful, but terrifying steep lanes where nothing can pass — except ghosts — roads that lead down to dead-ends by innumerable creeks.

I had to make for the metropolis of Lerryn, capital of the neighbourhood. I passed through the pretty village, with its pink and white-washed houses, its rivercraft, and over the hump of the bridge, one Sunday evening in the depth of the Cornish summer. The place was almost blotted out by blustering wind and rain. Fuchsias and blue hydrangeas strained at the leash like demented animals; the rain merged with the water in the creek overflowing at full floodtide.

Through the village, I took a turn off the main road up a steep narrow lane to the promised beacon of St Greep. Apprehensive as always in this country — for how could I reverse all the way down that twisting lane if I met anything? — I pushed on up, trumpeting at every corner like the coming of the Lord.

St Greep church passed in a storm of rain: the time of evensong, not a soul visible, but a burst of a solitary bell suddenly clashed into the ear and was gone. On I went until the road forked. I was to ignore the ironic notice 'One Way Street', go flat against it, down into and through a farm area and make a sharp left turn.

I obeyed, made a left turn: here was a renovated house with back-court of slate — should I follow the cart-track to the left? I looked, just in time, to see a precipice and the green sheet of water of the submerged creek before me. I asked my whereabouts of two upstanding youths, bareheaded in rain and wind, with something suggestively Arthurian about them. One was tall and black-haired, hair standing up straight and short-cropped; the other a fair Sir Galahad. The dark one took the lead and answered me with a foreign accent.

Backing away from the precipice, I made along the top of the creek to the recognisable declivity on the left, a white gate left open for me and into the quiet of the enchanted valley-bottom: a range of ancient farm-buildings, stones of the old monastic cell and chapel. I jolted along the rough drive to the Queen Anne farm-house facing the head of the creek, the sodden lawn and, beyond, the Monks' Walk along the edge of the moss-green water.

There on the steps in the rain, mackintosh huddled round shoulders, was the owner to greet me.

*

New to the place, he had already developed a fixation upon it. (Or had it upon him?) St Carroc's had got him. His inheritance of it was characteristically deviant, in the Cornish manner. In the Victorian age there had been two illegitimate descents in succession, the whole place going down gradually, outlying bits of land sold off, until only the valley-bottom was left, the house with its river-frontage and its memories.

Gawen was the last sprig of the old stock, a branch that had gone out to New Zealand in early days. Himself a promising young painter in London now, he had scraped together every penny to save the place from going out of the family at the end of the feckless line there.

Everything was to do. He couldn't afford to come down for more than a week or two, or a week-end, at a time; now he was anxious to show me what he had accomplished. Up over the rocky steps we went, into the back-court with the débris that had come to light from the monastic cell. Every scrap was precious to this passionate artist from so far away, whose deeper roots were nevertheless here. I glimpsed a holy-water stoup of rough granite, a bit of column with its capital that went back to Norman times. Various other bits and pieces were lying about; a shaped mullion, the head of a medieval or Tudor window — all precious as jewels to this scion of a newer world — the Long Cloud on the fringes of the Pacific.

We went inside. Gawen explained his plans. The dairy was to become the kitchen, the kitchen to become the dining room, screened off like a medieval hall. In the staircase-hall one could see that the house had been built for a family of gentlefolk; the staircase had style: wide-spread stairs with good low treads, twisting balusters carrying up to a spacious landing. On either side was a parlour, one with a painted corner-cupboard, which Gawen had already had copied for the hall. He had now completed the decoration of his front room, doing the painting himself.

He had gathered a great armful of foliage and flowers to take back with him to London. I was surprised at his going to so much trouble.

'I can't bear to leave the place,' he said. 'It's always like this when I'm going.'

He hadn't been off the premises the whole week he had been there. Out of doors he had been scything and mowing and weeding, carrying hay and burning up rubbish, seeing to the boat moored by the Monks' Walk; indoors he had been painting and furbishing, all on his own. He clearly needed someone to help him.

There he stood, six feet of him, tall and slender, rather lank dark hair, a curiously low voice with a tang of accent more colonial than Cornish. An appealing personality, not easy to penetrate, rather lonely this melancholy summer evening — and himself sad at leaving. Decidedly, he needed a helping-hand.

'Do you know the story of the crucifix that was found here, turned up in the soil like those carved stones at the door? I'm very anxious to see it. Wouldn't it be wonderful if it came back to where it belongs?'

I promised to look it up and tell him what I could find out at our next meeting. Myself away all winter in California, it was not until the next summer that we coincided in Cornwall again and I was able to tell him what I had learned.

*

The monastic cell — never more than a prior and a couple of monks there all through the Middle Ages, more often a prior with one young monk — had been founded by Robert of Mortain, half-brother of the Conqueror, who got the earldom of Cornwall at the Conquest and gave the cell to the abbey of Mont St Michel in Normandy.

Of course, the place went far back beyond the Normans to Celtic days and the Age of the Saints. Its origin was the holy well, a little way up the slope, a damp spot in Gawen's orchard. At the head of the creek the Saint and his disciples had erected a stone cross now in St Greep churchyard, removed in the Victorian age. Around it in succeeding ages were buried his faithful successors, Celtic hermits and medieval monks, under what is now Gawen's innocent front lawn, smooth and shaven.

Laurence Castletown was the last prior, accompanied to the end by his companion, a younger monk, James. Except for saying mass, hearing confessions, keeping the light before the Saint going — they were really a couple of farmers living off the soil like everyone else.

Mute and inglorious as their lives had been, they were not

going to see the end of all that century-long way of life without making their mute inglorious protest. When the monasteries were suppressed and sentence of expulsion passed upon the prior and his companion, they took the most cherished possession of their chapel, the gilt crucifix that stood on the desecrated altar, and buried it at night deep in the corner of the garth.

I have seen the crucifix, and a treasure it is — even if only of copper-gilt. It looked to me, on the sole occasion when I was allowed to see it, to be of the thirteenth century or early fourteenth century when the great John de Grandisson came from the Papal Court at Avignon to be bishop of Exeter and was a connoisseur of such things. It had an almost Spanish look — that deep Spanish sadness in the elongated face, the emaciation of the body. The early date of the work spoke in the flat treatment of the toes, the fingers of the outstretched hands.

What would I not give to possess this treasure, yielded up by the earth after some three hundred and fifty years of oblivion!

If this was how I felt about it, what would not Gawen feel about it when he saw it?

It had been dug up in the 1880's, in the corner where it had been buried in the 1530's. The farmer had been glad to part with it to the local landowner, a man of antiquarian tastes who appreciated it. It was now in the possession of his granddaughter, Fay Morgan, who had once let me see it.

Gawen, of course, was pining to get a glimpse of it.

*

I did not see him again for a year, and in the interval two developments had taken place.

Gawen's painting had flowered, he had found his own style and was beginning to be successful. He had found the means of expressing his own inner fantasy, his passion for the spirit of place, the life that houses live on their own when no one is looking, especially deserted houses where much has happened — one longs to know what — and of rendering their atmosphere. He had an exquisite sense of colour and line: he was a colourist and a *fantaisiste*.

Gawen had found himself, and his own true nature, in his work. He would be able to live more at St Carroc's.

And, besides, a much-needed helper had come to his aid there. Diego, the dark young Spaniard who had directed me on my first visit, had descended the hillside to take a hand in the operations that were too much for Gawen on his own. He was not only a good hand with a scythe but with a boat; like his namesake, the Apostle, he was a fisherman — expert at hoiking up trout from the river, or eels from the creek, and as expertly baking them. He was a good cook — which Gawen was not.

Diego developed a fixation on St Carroc's: it spoke to him as it spoke to Gawen. A native of Galicia, indeed of Santiago itself, Diego was of the same stock as the Cornish, dark, by turns melancholy and gay; above all, of the soil.

*

Meanwhile, what of the crucifix? How was Gawen to come by that?

He would have to make love to the aloof daughter of the lord of the manor. In a world falling all round her, she was rather upstage. Would he make a good impression?

Apparently he did, for she too was interested in the arts. She was only a year or two older than Gawen, and heart-free, her husband having been killed in the war. But she was not easy to please; and she was not giving herself away. Moreover, she possessed what Gawen very much wanted — the crucifix that belonged to St Carroc's.

There was some difficulty in bringing them together; but the lady came one afternoon to picnic on the lawn in front of

113

the creek. She came up the river alone, herself at the wheel of her motor-boat, painted green, the colour of the creek. The effect was striking; she was wearing a light green summer-dress: it seemed as if this vision arose from the water itself.

I had been asked to tea, and was suitably impressed by the elegance of her appearance. She was tiny, like a fairy-tale princess; but such was her poise, the curve of foot and instep, that she lost nothing in seductiveness or, more curiously, authority as she took possession of the lawn.

Diego moved about noiselessly, bringing the tea, handing the anchovies of his native Galicia. I, of course, was a mere foil.

She was talking to Gawen about the paintings at the Hall. (It was called 'Hall', as rarely in Cornwall: and was more like a Gothick castle out of Horace Walpole or Mrs Radcliffe.)

'You really must come and see the paintings one day — both of you.' It was kind of her to include me — she evidently meant me; but Diego was as clearly omitted.

'You know that Opie, before he left Cornwall, was taken up by my family. We've got several of his early paintings — two moonlight scenes by the sea-shore. Where do you suppose he can have got the idea? — an uninstructed peasant painting on his own down here in Cornwall. He can never have heard of Vernet, can he?'

'I don't suppose so. But his friend, Dr Wolcot, might well have had engravings. He was an amateur painter himself.'

'Oh, the horrid Peter Pindar, with his ballads against the ladies of Fowey!'

The conversation moved to another painter of moonlight scenes, the much less well known Patch.

Gawen had never heard of him.

The lady had. 'Didn't he have to live abroad for the good of his country?' she said disapprovingly, taking us all in at a glance.

I helped Diego to carry the tea-things in, while Gawen

demonstrated the Monks' Walk with its rare ferns to its rarer visitant. In the encouraging atmosphere of that green cloister he was able to raise the question of the crucifix and whether it might be allowed to revisit its old home too. The lady promised that she would bring it with her on her next visit.

I watched her departure, the vision melting into the water, one with the creek. 'Morgan le Fay', I registered.

*

I was not present on her second visit, neither was Diego. So it was not clear whether she succeeded in penetrating Gawen's defence, or to what extent, for something upset him and disturbed the peace of mind he needed for his work.

The lady had broken her word to bring the crucifix with her; and Gawen's disturbance of mind had something to do with that. The crucifix had become a symbol of the subterranean tension that had risen up between them. She had certainly managed to disturb the still waters of the creek.

On one side he was tempted; but was she desirable in herself?

Yes — oddly so. There was the fairy princess, smiling, intelligent, slightly mocking — out to seduce. She was very dark: black hair, with a rare tinge of rust in it. Her eyes seemed dark; they were certainly brown, but if you dared to look closer you saw that they belonged to the kind that have as much green as brown, a certain witchery. (Was she a witch, perhaps?)

Other things suggested themselves: an easy way of life, no more scuffling like the gulls in the creek for the garbage of critics' notice. She had possessions to offer, beautiful objects — the Hall was full of them. (Would there, however, be a way of escape?) The joys of family life — would they turn out to be so?

A choice was posed — a choice between two ways of life.

He could only decide for himself: no one could help him — at least no other human being. Something else came to his aid.

*

The crucifix came back to St Carroc's.

On her third visit, her third time of asking, the lady brought it with her. Perhaps she thought it would settle the issue — as, in the end, it did.

Gawen's eyes were filled with desire when, for the first time, he came face to face with it. But it was an unexpected, a strange, confrontation. Looking at it closely, taking the cold object into his warm hands, enfolding it, he ceased to want to possess it.

What he found was that, gazing at the weary lids of those half-closed eyes, the Oriental-looking slit of suffering beneath them, he himself was enabled to see more clearly. He saw himself as he was, accepted himself as he was, came to terms with himself.

He saw that renunciation was the path to fulfilment — renunciation of anything that distracted him from his work, however alluring or seductive, or whatever it promised. It was not all renunciation: he could enjoy those delights that were propitious to creation, whatever anyone else might think. He was not to live his life in the light of others' eyes.

He took a last look into hers — and saw that in their depths there was a gleam of red. A warning of danger? A suggestion of resentment, an affronted pride? Was she altogether human?

He looked at the downcast eyes of the figure on the cross — patience and suffering, a willed resignation to his own fate, not in accordance with another's will.

He hesitated no longer. In that moment the lady saw herself defeated.

Without a word she withdrew, like a ghost, from the house. The moon had come up over the creek; the tide was at the full, lapping at the Monks' Walk.

As she drew away in her boat, under the witchery of the
moon-laced trees, she took a dark object from her breast,
held it for a moment in full sight of the house, then threw it
into the shadowy waters.

It glistened in the moonlight for a flash as it fell, and
Gawen knew that he was free.

XIII

Night at the Carn

Carn means a rock or outcrop of rocks — a feature of the landscape in all Celtic countries. This particular Carn lay on the eastern edge of the china-clay massif of mid-Cornwall, upon which it turned its back, looking out across miles of untouched moor away to Brown Willy and Rowtor, and southwards down rumpled slopes to the coastal plain and the sea. These precipitous slopes, falling some eight hundred feet in a couple of miles had been streamed for tin since prehistoric times. Hence the full name of the place Carn Stents, which implied something to do with tinning.

The place was striking, sometimes beautiful, often forbidding, wreathed in mist or lashed by rain. It had a prehistoric feeling about it: one could imagine the creatures crouching in their pits and shacks, in the hollows of the moor. It was grim and gaunt, strangely thrilling, with the wild scents of the moor thrown up — camomile and tansy, whortleberries and bracken: a haunted place, withdrawn, keeping its own secrets, bewitching under the clear light of full moon, with sharp, unwavering shadows as if they looked straight at you.

The Carn itself was flat-topped, whether it had been weathered like that naturally, or scalped by human hands: it looked like a place for human sacrifice. One could imagine the smoke going up from that exposed altar on the rim of the horizon.

Beneath it there fell sheer on one side an old disused quarry, with deep pools of water in its green, translucent depths; under the rocks and stones squatted fat frightening toads, favourites with witches.

118

The water provided a supply for an improbable feature in this exposed and windy landscape: a garden as improbable as its creator. For it had been created around a modern house, plumb in a nest of rocks on a shoulder below the Carn.

The first problem had been to create shelter. Rocks had been cleverly moved to make little green rooms within which the rare scented azaleas and rhododendrons grew, with a carpet of rock daffodils putting out their blowing heads in earliest spring. Earlier still were the snowdrops, sprinkled like flakes of snow all over the place. Hedges of thick veronica and eschallonia were planted, fortified by thickets of bamboo — more green closes within which camellias would grow; in summer pools of sea-blue agapanthus lilies, set off by the innumerable scarlet bells of fuchsias.

Within these defences the garden's creator was able to use a level stretch for a long alley of grass, bordered by flowering cherries and autumnal sumach. This alley was pivoted upon, and led the eye to, an unexpected monument: an eighteenth-century chimney stack of a disused tin-mine. The eighteenth century could not make anything that was not honest and decent; the sturdy stone stack had good lines, not tall, the top finished off in brick, rust-colour now, while between the two was a shapely moulded cornice of granite. A perfect eye-catcher, as if a folly had been planned for the spot.

The place was a series of separate gardens that gradually took shape, marked off by natural rock, stone-built walls, or green fences of hardy flowering shrubs. In an enclosure below the house was a patch of white foxgloves set off by brilliant blue anchusa — an astonishing carpet of colour that caught the eye from the big living room of the house.

Though the house lived under almost perpetual siege from wind from one quarter or another, by any and every means it was kept at bay. The place was a paradise; but it needed courage to cope with it. And not only courage, but a certain exaltation of spirit, a loftiness of mind to be equal to it — I had almost said, to get even with it. I could never have contemplated living there: too high-minded, too noble, in epic or at least heroic mood.

I never felt at east there on my rare visits in youth, for all the good will and benevolence of my hosts. As one sat in that large room with the figured wall-paper, I noticed that panes of glass had been set in on either side of the chimney-piece to let in the view of the sea, six or seven hundred feet below. It was stupendous; it was too much. On the other side, looking towards the Stack, among the great rocks and boulders the house sat among the clouds, on a level with the westering sun.

One could never live up to such a habitation: it was hardly human.

*

This impression was fortified by its owners, whose creation it was.

Talk about going to the bad, *they* had gone to the good! Every conceivable form of good works was theirs — particularly Virginia's, for Matthew's chief activities were the garden, his painting and ceramics. Virginia was the politician and social worker, the local councillor sitting on innumerable committees, up to her eyes in public functions and engagements, exhausting her stock of robust good health in running her own house, entertaining everybody and helping the neighbours with their chores, if not their duties.

They both had money, and this, in the days between the two German wars, they regarded as a trust for the benefit of others.

It should be added that they were entirely English, not a drop of Cornish blood in either of them. Indeed their attitude to the Cornish, so kind, so benevolent, was really condescending. They found their neighbours, 'the locals', the subject for amusement, of supercilious jokes between themselves. They regarded our beliefs and prejudices, our precious foibles — by which we held on to some deeper experience of life than theirs — as comic 'superstition'. A couple of Cambridge intellectuals, they had grown up with the Bloomsbury lot. Foreigners in Cornwall, they might have been slumming.

Though I shared their Left Wing political views, when young, I didn't hit it off with them — and couldn't quite understand why. As I grew older I gave them a little of their own back. They laughed at the prejudices of the Cornish; very well: Virginia was an addict of the League of Nations Union. She would sally out in all winds and weathers to attend a pointless meeting of half-a-dozen faithful, or to start up some branch in an unlikely spot. So, in return for her reflections on the Cornish, I circulated a little *mot*:

> 'Virginia thinks that the League of Nations
> exists to support the League of Nations Union.'

They had a sense of humour like precious, but brittle, porcelain, and this was not very well received.

Virginia was very much concerned about the racial question — on which she failed to rally any enthusiasm on my part.

I said that I was afraid I didn't really qualify for the modern world:

'You see, I don't really believe that blacks are better than whites.'

This rather nettled her, especially coming from someone much her junior. She detected impertinence behind it. For her attitude to me was again protective, encouraging to a promising 'local', in short patronising. To me she was a kindly aunt: talk about an 'avuncular' attitude, hers could only be described as tantular.

As for the question of race — did it never occur to these two outliers of Bloomsbury living in our midst, that they were virtually encysted in a population of primitive country folk, who had inhabited these islands long before *their* ancestors

121

had crossed the North Sea from the mud-flats of Germany? Virginia and Matthew were themselves islanded amid a population of another race, who went back to the prehistoric camps, the dolmens and menhirs, the Carn itself, with its suggestion of louring rites.

There was the case of Crazy Eliza, for whom Virginia was for ever trying to arrange some good, to take her off to an establishment or home, give her a holiday in a seaside resort.

Eliza wouldn't have known what to do with herself, and got up to some mischief out of pure malice.

She lived all by herself in a shack — no more than a one-roomed hut with a lean-to — up by the Carn. I never rightly knew her story, and never saw her near enough to speak to. Every evening at sunset she would circle the moor, as if looking for something she had lost, clasping her arms and talking to herself.

As often as not her crazy course ended with a descent into the quarry. She gave a wide berth to anyone else out on the moor — visibility on every side; anyhow none of the local people would dream of interfering with her. She was known to be a witch, capable of ill-wishing you — no one wanted to be 'ill-wished'. Besides, it was well understood what her visits to the quarry were for: to select her toads for the venoms she brewed up. A toad was her familiar.

All this was wicked nonsense to Virginia — and all the wickeder for being nonsense.

'The poor woman just suffers from delusions,' she would say. Or, 'She's been persecuted: she just needs to be nursed back to sanity. She's normal enough underneath: she needs taking out of herself.'

And from time to time Virginia proceeded to take her out of herself, visiting the shack with some of her own concoctions — new-baked bread, quince-jelly, a cream-cheese.

*

Matthew kept out of all this, indeed out of most of Virginia's do-good activities. He was really sufficient to himself. I could never make out how they got married or why. It certainly was a curious relationship — more maternal on Virginia's part, I used to fancy. The marriage was naturally childless. The early Christian Fathers would sometimes try the flesh by sleeping with their wives, a drawn sword between them. Perhaps Matthew and Virginia slept with a four-tain pen between them.

Virginia had married off the rebound from an unhappy love-affair with a famous poet. She had grown up at Cambridge, a normal, conventional girl, not very clever, but in the centre of the intellectual set. The poet fell in love with her and insisted on her living with him. When she fell in love with him, he fell out, led her a tormented life and himself was killed in the first German war.

Matthew, the eldest son of a family with a large estate in East Anglia, was a very 'suitable' match for her, one up in social class. But he chose to slip the inheritance to a younger brother, to devote himself to his painting and his ceramics, and came to Cornwall to live his life his own way.

But why had he married?

He was a faun of a man, agile but undersized, leaping about the rocks of his garden like a sprite or an elf. He had come to Cornwall for the purity of the light for his painting — it was like his attitude to life, remote and pure, hardly human. He had settled on the edge of the china-clay district for the benefit of his experiments in ceramics. He had fixed on this site among the rocks below the Carn to create his garden.

He was a gifted man, but did he altogether add up?

It was impossible to maintain any free flow of conversation with him, for there was no *flow*, no communication. At some point it was dammed up; everything was censored, or at least filtered through that crystal-clear mind, tested by those cold, ice-blue eyes under the tousled, curly hair. The voice was cracked; one almost expected the ears to rise to a point.

Like Virginia, he was deliberately kind, benevolent, but one never came in touch with him. His sentences were brittle and staccato: I never heard him say anything longer than this once, showing us an antique cameo:

'In Victorian days described romantically as "Venus Ana-dyomene". Today described by Jackie Beazley as "Squat-ting Woman".'

One had the constant sense that one was failing him: one couldn't get up to him, let alone live up to him. He was like a bit of his own ceramics.

I had little sense in those days; all the same, I had an explanation of my own as to why things were as they were.

In my callow view, if Matthew had followed his own true nature, he would not have married at all. He had very little sex anyway. If he had felt free to follow his own inclinations, who knows where this would have led him? To the free-for-all of the School of Paris? Or the bourgeois Bohemianism of the artists of Newlyn or St Ives?

To Matthew, with his high Victorian background, such *dérèglement* was unthinkable. He made the sacrifice of his own nature to his principles: the strange impression of in-satisfaction his personality gave was the result.

The very last time I saw him, after Virginia had vanished from the scene and he was terribly alone, he was visibly glad to see me. Yet all he said, in that strained staccato voice, was:

'Any messages?'

For a moment I couldn't think what he meant. Then it flashed across my mind: were there any messages from the outside world?

I had to admit there were none.

His face fell.

I had failed him again.

*

124

I was away at the war when Virginia died, so I never did know the full story of it. But neither did anyone else: it was highly mysterious.

Matthew was away on war-work up the country. Virginia held the fort at home, wearing herself out with her war-work all over the county, on top of what she considered her duty to her own vicinity.

Actually, on the verge of a nervous breakdown, Virginia was under the doctor's care, and he had insisted on her going away for three months' complete rest. Moreover, he had put pressure on her to see that she went. He had made the arrangements, and the very next day, the first of the month, she was to leave for her holiday.

Old Eliza up at the shack was very ill, perhaps dying, and wanted someone to sit up the night with her. No one else would do it. They were, quite simply and honestly, afraid.

Virginia said that this was all nonsense, and that she would go and sit up with Eliza.

That night was a crisp, clear night of scintillating stars and, for a rarity, no wind. The wind had dropped, even around the Carn: you could have heard a cry for miles round, the cry of some animal dragged to its death by stoat or weazel, the bark of a fox, hoot of owl or croak of toad: all sounds were preternaturally sharp. So were the shadows.

Virginia set off with her basket, latching the gate under the twisted thorntrees and making up the rough path to the Carn, up that heaving breast of hill under the stars.

As she stumbled up among the loose stones, it came to mind that tomorrow, when she would be going away, was the first of November: All Saints day. This then was All Hallows' E'en, when spirits were said to walk: the old folk hereabouts believed that they came out of their graves on this night of the year, walked about the earth and vanished at cockcrow.

What nonsense they believed, Virginia registered. All the

same, a cold spasm clutched her heart when she saw a large toad squatting at the threshold of the shack.

What happened that night in the course of Virginia's night-watch no one knew.

It was not the old crone who died, but Virginia. . . .

*

There was a good deal of rumour in the district at the time. Some people thought that Virginia had been deliberately frightened to death, the victim of some malicious prank. (It would have been a not unimaginable return for her good works, among some people in some circumstances).

But most folk felt sure that the witch had put a spell upon her, a trance that Virginia never came out of.

There had, of course, to be a coroner's inquest. But it was at one of the worst moments of the war, and everybody was anxious to get the incident out of the way.

No sense could be got out of the old crone as to what did happen that night. She was out of her mind — or pretended to be. And not long after she made a death of it.

Matthew returned from the war a shadow of his former self, to stretch out his hand to a shade, and lived not long.

The house was taken over by strangers in the post-war years. They proposed to chicken-farm on the lower slopes towards the tin-streamed valley. This was a failure.

No one could keep going Matthew's exquisite creation, the enchanted garden in that impossible situation, with all its rarities needing such loving care and attention as he had lavished upon it. The genius of the place had gone; the *genius loci* had taken over.

When I went by the deserted place on a brief visit to Cornwall not long ago, the garden was all overgrown: ubiquitous bracken a foot high taking over, heather, brambles, wild convolvulus with its wicked white trumpets blaring triumph.

With Virginia the Carn had won.

With Matthew's garden the moor too would win.

XIV

The Beneficent Shoes

Everybody said they were a very nice young couple. And so they were. They were, as everyone remarked, ideally suited to each other. They were both school teachers. They had met at Plymouth, where he had been a master in a big boys' secondary school, while she was a mistress in the girls'. So they had that community of interest which everyone assures us is the foundation of a successful marriage.

Not less important, they were in other respects mutually complementary. She was the active, practical spirit who managed the house and, in effect, their joint career. But she had decided to subordinate her own career to his: when he obtained the headship of a small secondary school in mid-Cornwall, she married him.

He was the more interesting character, though a less good teacher. Where she was direct and forcible, with a clear head and way of explaining things, he was diffident and oblique in his approach — an unsympathetic observer would say at first, a little confused. Which was not quite true: it was just that he was aware, perhaps of more things at once than either Jane or the unsympathetic observer. He had a natural distinction of mind, which somehow his curious fits of absent-mindedness did not impair, but rather enhanced. And there went along with this an unmistakable goodness of nature, a sympathy of temper which could be felt rather than expressed.

Not that Jane had not a real goodness of heart too, but hers was a thoroughly practical nature. She was English. He was Cornish — or rather half-Cornish, which added to the indecisions, the impreciseness of his mind, and perhaps accounted for those quivering antennae of sensibility which were not easily observable to some people. He came of farmer stock and had a good Cornish name: Dennis Tristain. (One wishes Cornish people would draw more upon the lovely names they have coming down from their remote past: Mark, Gawain, and Tristram; Perran, Petrock, and Geraint.)

They had already settled into a house which suited them very well. It was not an old house — one of those dank, grey Cornish houses which are inevitably associated with the idea of ghosts. Jane would not have held with such ideas anyway. She would have regarded them as illusions, for which her practical mind had no use. Dennis — though he, too, if asked direct, would probably have agreed that they were illusions — instinctively knew the hidden truth, and with a native Cornish caution would have given the universe the benefit of the doubt.

Anyhow, their house, so far from being large and gloomy and at the end of a long, dark drive of rhododendrons and ilexes, was small and gay and at the end of a short straight drive in from the main road. It was built, like a good many modern houses in Cornwall, after a manner brought back from overseas, from South Africa or Michigan or Montana, with which Cornish folk have had so many mining connections in the past: that is to say, it was practically a bungalow, with verandahs all round. Very agreeable, since it had a good view of the sea, with the lizard-like neck of the headland, as of some great primitive animal, closing their seaward view.

All that they knew of the history of the house was that it had been built by a mining captain, who had returned having 'made his fortune', but with the hand of the miners' phthisis heavy upon him. The captain was a laconic bachelor of whom people knew little; he had been looked after by an elderly 'person', a little lame, who kept herself very much to herself and was his housekeeper. He died, and she died shortly after.

128

The Beneficent Shoes

The house was so up-to-date that it had not even a horseshoe over the door — as every Cornish house should have — to bring its inmates good luck, as we say nowadays, or, as the older folk know, to keep witches out. Dennis a little regretted this, as he had a feeling for the ancient ways of his people; but he knew that any attempt to rectify the omission would be regarded with little patience by Jane. So the house went unprotected.

Jane liked it there: it was a pleasurable experience to direct her undoubted talent for running things (and people) into a new channel. Dennis afforded her plenty of scope. He was the untidiest person in the world: a charming disorder naturally arose all round him. Books piled themselves up on the floor wherever he was; papers, newspapers, journals, reports accumulated on his writing-desk and so snowed him under that there was no writing at it; the particular paper he was in need of at the moment had a way of hiding itself in the mass, into which Dennis would plunge hopelessly, helplessly, a puzzled look in those sloe-black eyes with the curious almond shape. Jane was very fond of him, especially at such moments: she took him in hand. She had a favourite epitaph for him, with which she used to tease him; there would be found inscribed upon his tombstone, she said, the words 'He never shut a drawer'.

In some months of married life Dennis was making good progress in the art of shutting drawers and replacing books on shelves, when his incurable forgetfulness seemed to break out in another direction. He could never be sure where he had put his shoes: they always seemed to be turning up somewhere other than where he thought he had left them.

'Where have you put my shoes, darling?' he would say sweetly, wandering rather disconsolately round the house after Jane.

'I haven't seen them,' she would say. And then add: 'Anyone would think that they had walked off of themselves — the way you mislay them about the place.'

Dennis did indeed think there was something odd about the way they turned up in the most unexpected corners, where he felt he had never left them. But he owned many pairs of shoes, large and comfortable, mostly rather old and well-worn, inclined to be a bit 'trolled-over', as we say; and he could never be *quite* sure: he knew his own absent-minded ways too well. So he said nothing to Jane, who would have laughed at him for his pains.

When the confusion became too insistent to avoid notice, she introduced a rule. Dennis was to keep his shoes in order in the back kitchen — that is to say, those pairs which he wasn't using at the moment.

One day, not long after this measure of reform, Dennis came home from school, changed into his slippers in the kitchen, leaving his out-door shoes there, went down to their bedroom for a book, read for a little, wandered into his study and out again into the sitting-room, where a cheerful fire was burning and Jane had the tea ready — to find that his shoes were waiting for him beside his drawn-up chair in front of the fire.

'Thank you, darling,' he said. 'I didn't know that they were wet.'

'What is?' said Jane, her mind concentrated on pouring out tea with one hand and fetching out a plate of hot scones with the other.

'My shoes,' said he contentedly, helping himself to a scone.

'But, my dear, I haven't touched them,' said Jane, paying attention once more.

'You must have done,' said Dennis, opening incredulous eyes.

Jane caught the look in his eyes, and answered shortly, 'What nonsense! You know perfectly well you must have put them there yourself to dry.'

'I did not,' he began; 'I could swear that I took them off in the kitchen and left them there.' Having said as much for himself, he then began to wonder. Had he after all taken them off in the kitchen? The strange chord deep down in his consciousness – something lost in his early experience – which was aroused whenever he contemplated his own forgetfulness, vibrated with uncertainty. He was no longer sure. Perhaps he had taken his shoes off in the bedroom and brought them up with him? But he distinctly remembered sitting down on a chair in the kitchen and taking them off there. On the other hand, that might have been yesterday. What was he doing yesterday? His mind, wandering down those familiar corridors of the research into memory, lost control of the situation.

Jane, with her woman's instinct, realised that and resumed it into her own hands. She said affectionately, 'Really, darling, anybody would think it was someone else walking round the house in your shoes.'

He was defeated. She made the defeat palatable by handing him the plate in her most seductive manner: 'Denny, dear, have another scone. They're a great success today. I'm really rather proud of them.'

He looked down at the shoes. They looked up at him in a faithful, mute, protesting way, as if to say they were at his service, however much they might be disregarded, discountenanced, in other quarters.

He understood the look. It was lost on her. At the same moment he had that curious experience which we all know well: of having been through it all before on some previous occasion. He felt, as he sat there, that he had been sitting there before just like that, wrangling with Jane about those shoes; there was the plate of scones, there were the shoes looking up at him, the same thought passing through his head, and he had heard her – oh so clearly, so insistently, before – saying just those words: '*Anybody would think it was someone else walking round the house in your shoes.*'

Though his was a poetical mind, it was also not without

logic; and he found himself thinking: 'But the shoes were not wet at all, so I couldn't have put them there to dry.'

He was now quite certain in himself. But he said nothing to Jane: there were things that that admirable clear mind could not conceive. It was the first time that he perceived at all clearly its limitations. He had been content to repose entirely upon her practical capacity, her better judgment. He was now not so sure. This was the first time they had had anything approaching a tiff. She had won, as was to be expected; but all the same, she was not right. It was a very small matter; but it is precisely upon such small matters that a widening rift in sympathies is revealed. The matter dropped between them.

Some months later Dennis' sister was married from the house. (She was his only sister, and their parents were no longer alive.)

Jane was absolutely at her best in these proceedings, took charge of her sister-in-law, made most of the arrangements about her trousseau, and, with the aid of her faithful attendant Mrs Honey — whose sole ambition in life was to have her good Cornish name, which we all know how to pronounce, pronounced Hony to rhyme with bony, stony, or phoney — cooked the wedding luncheon. Jane entered thoroughly into the spirit of a Cornish wedding, and was willing to aid Judy in her determination not to omit a single customary propriety. The bride, according to custom, must wear one piece of clothing which was old and another which was borrowed. Mrs Honey produced an old garter and Jane lent Judy a petticoat for the occasion.

Dennis, for his part, was determined not to omit the proper rite of throwing an old shoe for luck after the departing couple.

They lingered long over their excellent luncheon; and when the car finally drove off down the drive on the way to their honeymoon, the winter's day was drawing in. It was growing dark. Dennis followed the car down to the gates, and as it turned in the main road, took a good straight aim with his old shoe. The shoe hit the back wheel hard and rebounded like a boomerang. A handkerchief waved from the car, the white ribbons fluttered; they were off and away.

What followed was quite incredible. It was incredible to Dennis, who could hardly believe his own eyes. He was acquainted with the theory of boomerangs; he was interested in folklore. But neither of these interests had prepared him to see that shoe returning up the drive with him. It was between the two lights; it was growing darker every second. But there was enough light for Dennis to see that the shoe was not travelling in a straight line like a boomerang, but that it was trudging faithfully, convincingly up the drive step by step, as if alternating with another step that could not be seen: the shuffling gait of a tired elderly person, which was yet indefatigable, undiscouraged. There was something touching about that solitary step. One would say it was the walk of a woman, a little lame.

Dennis was not exactly frightened, for there was nothing malevolent about it: rather the contrary, it gave an impression of an unwearying, an unselfish devotion — something wholly beneficent. Yet he felt all his sensibilities become acute and tingling; his nerves thrilled; he felt that unmistakable sensation you have when your hair begins to rise and stand up on end. Never had he taken a walk that was so long as those few steps up the drive. Yet he could do nothing, did not wish to do anything. It was just as if he had been mesmerised.

When he got back to Jane and they went indoors together, she could see that something very odd had happened to him. And this time he told her, without any reserve.

She looked at him for a bit, and then burst into a peal of sound hearty laughing:

'Denny, darling,' she said, 'd'you know, you are quite, *quite* tight.'

She thought him, helpless as he was, utterly charming. Nothing would persuade her to the contrary − she was that sort of woman; nothing but ocular demonstration. And that was not very long in coming.

A fortnight after the wedding, on Twelfth Night, they were thinking of going down to the little church − the spire could be seen among the trees between the house and the sea − where a Nativity play was to be performed in place of the usual evensong. They were in a hurry to put the tea-things away, and had almost finished when they saw something very odd indeed. They quite distinctly saw a pair of Dennis' shoes walk slowly but doggedly across the room to the corner where they were washing up − pause, as if expecting some notice to be taken, and then return to where they had started from.

Their hearts stood still. They looked at each other; it was as if the scales had fallen from Jane's eyes and she saw further into the depths of Dennis' personality than she had ever seen before. She felt, for the first time, uncertain of herself, horribly uncertain. She went very pale and thought for a moment she was going to faint. She was visibly shaken. Dennis put an arm round her and led her into the sitting-room where she lay down for a bit on the sofa.

'What does it mean?' were her first words when she came round and recovered her self-control.

'I don't know,' was all Dennis could say. And then he remembered that he had recognised the same character, the same personality (so to say) in the steps: far from malevolent − kindly, wanting to be of service, as of some woman, ageing, but unwearied in doing good.

'I'm sure they mean nothing bad to us,' he added. 'Did you notice one thing about them, darling? They were the steps of someone a little lame?'

Jane had noticed: there was nothing that she had not observed now that at last she had seen for herself. She was more than willing now to credit what had happened to

134

Dennis in the drive on the evening of the wedding, and the other oddities that had occurred in his behaviour.

But what did it mean? That was the question that bothered them both. They did not go to church that evening; they stayed at home discussing it. They wanted to get it clear.

It was a decidedly queer experience; nothing that they had come across — or even read of — corresponded with it. They were a modern-minded young couple, intellectually open to conviction; and they were quite *au fait* with ghost stories — liked them in a superior way, a sort of pleasant titillation of the imagination.

It had never occurred to either of them to credit that *these things might happen*. They were willing to go as far as to allow that there might be something in an atmosphere. Where people had been through an intense experience, had been very unhappy, for example, that might leave some impress of the experience in the atmosphere of a room, a house where it had taken place. What had not occurred to their minds was that the same might be true of a place or a house where someone had been very happy, to which some-one was very attached. And that it might be something more than mere atmosphere.

Such was the upshot of their discussion. Not very satis-factory, and inconclusive, as all such discussions are.

A more practical upshot was that Jane was determined to leave the house.

Dennis was at bottom a little shocked that Jane, who had been so insentient, so unimaginative at first, should take it so badly when brought face to face with the facts. The facts were not at all frightening, he assured her. After all, it was certainly a benevolent ghost that haunted the house. It was the first time the word had been uttered between them. The assurance carried no weight with her. She was as obstinate now as she had been incredulous and positive at first. Was this a further-widening in the rift of sympathy between them?

135

Dennis gave way to her desire to leave the house. But before going, he determined to explore the facts as far as he could.

The facts were few. There was nothing very much to know. Merely that the previous occupant, a man dying slowly of the 'miners' complaint', had been looked after, people said, by a countrywoman who had come down there from the uplands — the great mass of moor and heath above the town. That she was a kindly person who, in spite of her lameness, dragged herself round to the last with cups of tea and hot-water bottles and medicine, fetching and carrying for the shy reserved sort of man who treated her with respect and consideration. Never a complaint. She once told someone that the happiest years of her life were those she passed there. Hers had not been a happy life. She had been stricken with serious illness when young, which had left her lame. Her mother had made her give up the young man who wished to marry her — as a matter of duty. After her parents' death she had lived a lonely life on her small-holding up in the hills. It became too much for her to carry on by herself, and she came down to the town to seek employment. All that she wished was to help others, and that she did until she died.

These were the facts, few and simple and kindly. But what was the explanation?

In this realm where there are no explanations, one can only ask questions. If only the young couple were wise enough to let her ghost help them in her way? . . . Was that what she wished? Since they were not, must she still go dragging her steps around those passages, until someone comes who will understand and accept unquestioning and without apprehension the willing service of those faithful feet?

136

XV

The End of the Line

It was the sight of the heron rising soundlessly from the marshes, its great wings moving slowly over the reeds, long legs trailing out behind, that woke him to normal consciousness and brought him back to the sense of his whereabouts. He remembered that the heron was the crest of the ancient family, now extinct, that had ruled for centuries in these parts, leaving its mark everywhere about, in the churches, the remote villages, the very look of the landscape. It was an odd thing to recall him to the everyday world after the strange experience he had been through, the shock he had received.

He remembered that he had been walking down the railway line, that curved round winding down the valley, it seemed hours ago, when it could only have been a matter of minutes, perhaps seconds − who could tell, in an experience lifted quite out of the run of the normal, as if on another plane of existence, giving a glimpse into what?

It was a summer evening, 'between the two lights', as we used to say in the West, when he set off from his comfortable Anglers' hotel − after a day's unsatisfactory fishing − for a break before a late dinner. He went down the disused railway line, lost in rumination and inner worry, impossible to disengage oneself from in the circumstances of the time.

What was he thinking about? − difficult to say as he only half took notice of the coloured flowers lighting up the sombreness of the track. There was brilliant, lemon-yellow toadflax, the rich gold of ragwort, pink willow-herb growing everywhere over the disused sidings. Sunk in reverie he was unaware of the sheep bleating up on the hillsides, the stag-horned oak at the curve of the line.

Suddenly all his senses were shocked into abnormal awareness. Round that very curve a train was approaching, not very fast, but with the bustling, determined 'chug-chug' of the old steam-engines coming up an incline.

At the same moment − or so it seemed − he saw a figure leap from the train at the bend, to fall broken against a gate barring an approach to the track at that point. Unmistakably the figure of a woman.

At the same moment − for everything had the illusion of simultaneity in this freak experience (was it dream or nightmare, or was he sleepwalking?) − he *heard* the jamming on of brakes, the hissing of escaping steam from the chugging engine. He noticed the glint of burnished copper on its dome; he *smelt* the cindery smell of the coal it consumed. All his senses were alerted; his hair stood on end as he saw figures descend from the train, the guard jump down from the running-board to investigate.

There had been an accident.

He hurried forward in the twilight, sensible enough to get off the track, sprinting alongside of the sleepers, to where the track curved round.

Arrived at the spot − there was nothing there! No figures, no body fallen at the foot of the gate, no train! *Silence* − it was that more than anything else that shattered his nerve, his confidence in his own sensations. He had so certainly heard the hiss of the escaping steam.

With the shocked awareness of a somnambulist he registered what he did see, with eyes opened. There were, of course, no sleepers on the track: they had long ago been taken up: so there could have been no train!

Yet here he was now at the curve in the line − there was the gate against which the woman's body had fallen.

The End of the Line

With the strange sharpness with which one takes note of an irrelevant detail in coming round from an injury, concussion or loss of consciousness, he looked up at the gate and read a notice long out of date:

The Railway Executive
Notice. By 8 Vic. Cap 20 Section 75
any person not fastening this gate having
passed through is liable to a fine of
forty shillings.

The poor woman − or lady, rather − who had fallen from the train had not 'passed through' − or had she? − she would not be liable to a fine of forty shillings − forty shillings was quite a sum in those early days of the reign of Queen Victoria. His mind was racing: really, he was going dotty. He must pull himself together.

It was at that moment that the heron rising from the marshes recovered him to ordinary consciousness and helped him to re-establish his whereabouts.

They were the same as in the nightmare, or hallucination, he had been through. He was still at the curve in the line. He now saw that there was a white gate on either side of the track, giving access to a lane that crossed at that point and went on down to a bathing place on the river. Though he could not see them he heard the voices of boys bathing there in the evening, shrill piping cries on the air.

Numbed with shock, feeling a little cold − utterly dumb-founded, not frightened in any way, but with inner anxiety increased along with confidence in himself and certainty of the validity of his own experience undermined, he retraced his steps up along the track to the hotel that had once been the Railway Hotel.

Nearby was the derelict station, signals removed and indeed anything of any value in the way of metal. He kept inside the

139

platform, for he noticed that the stone kerb along which the trains had drawn up was cracked and unsafe.

Here had been the Parcels Office, lower panes of glass in the windows broken, the upper still intact. Here was the waiting-room that had seen better days, had once been smart — for the station was little more than a halt, called into existence for the convenience of the family through whose property the little valley-line had passed. There was still timber from the woods usefully stacked on the side opposite the derelict platform, with its gaping holes of windows and broken glass.

It was the end of the line.

*

What was the explanation, if any, of the angler's unprecedented experience? He was a middle-aged man, rational enough in his way, not given to imaginative adventures. But, with the don's vested interest in knowledge, he was not satisfied to let the experience pass without seeking some explanation.

It took him a little time before getting on the track; people were reluctant to answer direct queries, in the West Country way, but he was a local man himself, at least by origin, and patiently he put the pieces together into a pattern.

*

Lost in the depths of the dark woods that covered the slopes and hills on the opposite side of the valley was a country house that had been left to the Historic Houses Trust by its last owner, an elderly maiden lady, Miss Pompilia Plumptre. She had no relations, no kith or kin, to whom to leave the place.

When Luke took advantage of his membership of the Trust to visit the house, he was somewhat surprised to find how little 'historic' it was. No Elizabethan or Georgian mansion, it was an extremely plain Regency house, hipped up on a terrace, like a railway platform, its only decoration a grand portico of Corinthian columns at the entrance.

The interior was all the more entrancing, and gave an extraordinarily strong impression of its last owner, as if it were only yesterday that she had ceased to live there – almost as if she might come back at any moment.

The whole of the furnishings were, unexpectedly, nineteenth-century: nothing earlier than Regency, some of the tables recognisably William IV, most of the furniture early Victorian. The whole place had been decorated and furnished by Miss Plumptre's grandparents, the builders of the house.

There were the elegant Wedgwood plaques of the grandparents in the entrance hall; within the fine staircase hall a *savonnerie* carpet woven with the family crest of the heron at each corner. The grand feature of the house was a series of three noble rooms *en suite*, opening upon each other, with only a couple of *scaliogla* columns at the divide, to form one gallery of a room, splendidly lit by tall Regency windows giving on to the raised terrace. (A notice, however, warned visitors not to venture upon it as unsafe.)

What was so agreeable was the lightsomeness, the livability, of it all – as against the sombre grandeurs of more historic houses, panelled glooms, heavily depending decorated ceilings, dark and awkward corners. Here all was light and airy, the branching chandeliers adding the glitter of their prisms and chains of cut glass drops.

It did not take him long to discern that everywhere was the impress of the personality of the last owner. On a little Victorian whatnot was a photograph of Miss Pompilia as a girl, straw-hatted and bee-line-waisted, with her pony, 'Czar'. On the chimney piece, there she was in the full array, ivory satin with a train, of her presentation-dress – presumably at one of the afternoon parties at Buckingham Palace that were substituted in Queen Victoria's widowhood in place of a full Court.

A round library table was covered with albums of family photographs from the days when there had been a family — doting parents, father the last baronet with bonneted, invalid wife, often out of doors, huddled in rugs. The daughter, evidently the light of their lives, appeared always healthy and vigorous. All through her later occupancy it would seem that she remained so, for the house was filled with mementoes of her activity and interests.

She had travelled a good deal over the empty years, for there was cabinet upon cabinet filled with her collection of marine shells. In earlier centuries the family had had a strong naval inflexion, and this came out in its last descendant's collection of ships' models filling a whole corridor beside the hall.

The long suite of rooms gave the strongest impression of her personality — the cases of exotic birds and butterflies between the windows, the tables decorated with Chinese jade; other tables packed with snuff-boxes from all over Europe, the fireplaces blocked out with painted trays, cabinets spread with decorative fans.

The whole place was a Victorian treasure-house, monument to the tastes — and the activity — of its last occupant.

But wasn't there a certain restlessness evident in it all? — Luke wondered, as he roamed round, fascinated, bent on gaining an insight into the character of the lonely woman who had so dominated her environment. Wasn't there a kind of insatisfaction that he discerned beneath the restlessness?

Why had she never married? Why had she not done her duty by carrying on the family, of which she evidently had so strong a sense and of which she exhibited — more tenaciously than her rather feeble parents — the inherited characteristics?

It took Luke a little longer, and some imagination, to penetrate the inwardness of her story — for, of course, there was one — and to light upon the explanation of her end.

*

She had, in fact, wanted to marry, and there had been somebody ready to marry her. But the young man had no money or position of his own — an impecunious rector's son on her estate — and was not on her level, heiress of the Plumptres.

Nevertheless, she had been in love with him, after her fashion, which was rather a patronising one.

She did not meet him openly, socially. Sometimes of an evening she would ride down the lane to the gate that gave on to the railway crossing — the lane went on to the bathing place on the river. She never went as far; she halted at the gate and never passed it.

There, in the shade and the obscurity of the dwarf-oaks, hazels and overhanging elder-bushes, their devious and oblique assignations took place.

She herself was tortured by a doubt: like many rich women in that day and age, when class-divisions were both subtle and firm, she felt that he was after her for her money. She knew she was not good-looking: she had vivacity, not charm; she had something of a masculine streak — indeed she had already the complex well-formed within her that she should have been the son and heir to carry on the name.

The rector's son had the more feminine charm, but, unsure of himself, was slow to make a declaration.

This, in itself, she thought a suspicious circumstance, where it was only deference.

She practically forced a proposal out of him; then, when it came — with the paradoxical turn of a spoiled and wilful only child — she rejected it.

She expected another, which she would accept — having tried him and tested his sincerity, as she thought. But he, more sensitive and easily discouraged, took it to heart. He went abroad, and shortly died.

Egoist as she was, she took this as final evidence of his sincerity and laid the grief to her heart. Not wanting in candour – she had the qualities of her defects – she blamed herself, rightly, and grieved for him all her life.

*

On succeeding to her father – her mother long since dead – as squire of the parish and indeed of several other parishes in the vicinity where her estates lay, she devoted herself to them and became a model landowner.

She made the well-being of her tenantry her prime concern; she built a number of up-to-date cottages on each one of her estates – not without more interference with their private concerns than her tenants altogether relished. (A Queen Victoria in her own domain, she was quite unaware of this, or of what was said of her behind her back).

She encouraged sewing and knitting classes, and even artwork, among the not too appreciative girls; she founded a Young Farmers' Institute for the young men. She kept a weather-eye open to their morals: no farms of hers were let to those of ill, or dubious, repute. She was very good to the poor.

A great lady in her region, rich and consequently respected, she could afford to indulge her whims and fancies. And this she increasingly did as she grew older. All power corrupts, we are told; and as her reign grew longer, solitary, with no one to check her, she became odder and more eccentric.

Some of her doings and sayings made history in her part of the West Country.

'When in doubt,' she asserted, 'I always say, "Plant an avenue!"'

As if one could. . . . She, however, was in a position to do so, and on each of her estates she proceeded to plant – on that where she resided an avenue of monkey-puzzles, for example, the only one of its kind in the West Country.

One or two of her richer neighbours sought to emulate her and plant an avenue; but, naturally, when carried out it was not quite right in her eyes.

Though much-travelled abroad, whence she brought back shells and *bric-à-brac* for her collections, she never acquired much skill in foreign tongues — another rather masculine trait. Somewhere in the French provinces she picked up the word '*pendule*' — she always applied it to the little gold-and-diamond watch that, depending on the end of a chain, was tucked in bee-line waist-band or pinned on unobtrusive bosom. It was always referred to as her '*pendule*'.

She had no idea that the county laughed at her for that, as for others of her little ways.

Any more than the county had any idea of the secret grief gnawing at her heart, or the surprise she was planning for them.

Hope springs eternal in the human breast, where money or property is concerned. One or two of her neighbours had been not without hope when they reflected that there was no heir to the Plumptre estates; as time went on and she became more eccentric they re-doubled their attentions.

She was not taken in: inner grief had left her singularly clear-eyed and without illusions about the outer world.

Her attentive neighbours, remote in their country fastnesses, were equally unaware of the new institution come to birth, in a very small way, the Historic Houses Trust: portent of an age to come.

She would give it its biggest lift yet, its effective start, a real foundation for the future, with the bequest of the whole of the Plumptre estates.

This took many consultations with her lawyers and the incipient Trust, much planning and forethought, a number of visits down the line — virtually her private railway-line — to the county town. On all these business matters her mind was as clear as a bell.

Inwardly, as the business drew to an end, her grief consumed her.

What was the point of going on?

Some purpose in her unfulfilled life was fulfilled. Why prolong the time of waiting?

The gate at the turn in the railway-line — that had been a turning point in her life — always had a fascination for her. She never failed to register its significance as the train passed it by. Once and again the train halted at that point, and the spot drew her.

One evening, returning from the city, there was a halt, and on the evening air she heard the voices of children calling her, at the same moment as a heron — with its own significance for her — rose above the marshes.

All things were coming together, she thought, alone in her private carriage, on the last of her visits to the city, when all the documents had been signed, sealed and delivered.

'And all things shall be well,' she said. On reaching the so much desired gateway she leaped.

She was the end of the line.

XVI

The Red Bicycle

The composer who was to become so famous — with a whole
festival devoted to his work on the south coast, and the international *réclame* proper to a Leftist — nearly lost his footing
on the way up. And this was how.

One fine spring evening he happened to be attending a
meeting inside Hyde Park, addressed by one of his favourite
Communist or near-Communist orators. He was not precisely
'attending', for his wandering eye lighted upon a very person-
able youth nearby — well-grown, dark, ivory skin, and those
lavender-blue eyes that go remarkably well with a dark
complexion.

The susceptible musician was much taken with this entrancing spectacle, but for all his efforts to attract attention
his fixed look received no notice. Or so it seemed. The handsome youth was much more attentive to the orator. Then the
musician noticed that squashed against the boy's legs was a
bicycle, a red bicycle. Those were the days when telegraph-
boys were provided with red bicycles. Evidently a telegraph-
boy.

Having had no success for all his devotion, Jonathan
Prickett — verging on early middle age, lean and lithe and
spry, though balding a little — decided to give up and left the
arena, that free-for-all exchange of nonsense.

Keeping a wary eye open — and he had a very wary, bright
eye indeed, a bold blue — he safely crossed the whirlpool of
traffic at Marble Arch and was going along the pavement
into Oxford Street, when a red bicycle came alongside and

147

stopped some yards ahead. The rider proceeded to fiddle with his lamp.

Mr Prickett, experienced and fly in these matters, took no notice and went on ahead of the stationary bicycle.

Some yards further ahead the bicycle stopped again. More fiddling with it.

At that Mr Prickett said, when he came ahead:

'You having trouble with your bicycle, sonny?' Mr Prickett was something of an Edwardian dandy, and affected the manner of speech of that free-and-easy age, when a good time was (or could be) had by all.

'Yes, something wrong with my lamp.'

Lighting-up time was approaching.

'Have you far to go?', inquired Mr Prickett kindly.

'Yes, all the way to Battersea,' said the youth.

'Wouldn't you like to come in with me and have something warm before you go on?'

The lad expressed no surprise at the invitation, rather welcomed it.

Mr Prickett's flat was not far away, cutting a sharp corner or two. They soon arrived. They went in, the boy leaving his red bicycle up against the railings outside the door.

*

They were indoors, comfortably sharing Mr Prickett's double-bed, and had reached mutual understanding – Johnny and Cyril to each other – when Jonathan's nosy house-keeper came to the door, and knocked loudly, enough to waken them *if* they had been asleep:

'There's a policeman downstairs at the front door to see you, sir.'

'My God, that's torn it,' Mr Prickett thought. 'That's the end of everything – career and all.' And he was to dine with a royal Duke of his acquaintance next week, on his way up!

He thought rapidly. 'Tell him I'm in the middle of dressing

148

for the Opera.' He was indeed undressed. 'I won't be five minutes.'

A very quick and experienced dresser, it was not much more than five minutes before he was on his way down, opera-cloak over his internal disarray, to meet his fate.

'Well, officer,' he said to the constable, 'what is it? Anything I can do for you?'

Mr Prickett's manner was of the most propitiating; some people said that he was irresistible, blue eyes and all — *when* he turned on the charm. The police-constable, however, did not appear to notice the double-talk, the suggestion in 'What can I do *for you?*'

Bluff and kindly, he said, 'I want to tell you that that there bicycle might easily be stole: you ought to take it inside.'

'Thank you very much,' said Mr Prickett, 'I will.'

He was still more grateful to observe that, in the gathering dusk, it was not noticeable that the bicycle was red.

'Phew!' said Mr Prickett with relief, as he returned upstairs. 'That was a narrow shave.'

In his agitation he had forgotten to give the constable anything for his kindly thought.

Mr Prickett was rather a mean man about money; not with his favours, where he was generous enough.

*

He and Cyril, who knew the score very well, came to a good understanding. They would meet again, and did from then on, at not too infrequent intervals.

Mr Prickett thought it best to put it on a regular basis and make a friend of Cyril, who for his part was very willing. For that, it was in the long run, better to know his family.

So, inquiring the lad's address, he made his way down to Battersea to call on them.

Cyril's father was — 'Of all things,' said Mr Prickett to a

friend some years after − a collector of night-soil. But they were respectable people − Catholics, as it happened.

Mr Prickett arrived at a gloomy tenement building and up a lot of steps, to be greeted at the door by Cyril's mother. 'Come in, and have a cup of tea,' said she, favourably impressed by the appearance of the gentleman, as to whom − or, rather, his kindness − they had been alerted by Cyril.

He was not present, but a couple of strapping boys, his brothers, were at table. Mr Prickett diverted his eye away from them, to concentrate all his charm on Mother.

'I was thinking,' said he, at length before going, 'that it might be a good thing for Cyril to get some fresh air in the country. I have a little cottage down by the Thames − it would be very good for him; he could get in some swimming too − perhaps help me with the garden.'

Nothing could be more agreeable, from everybody's point of view. And so it was arranged, and stood.

*

A more difficult step to negotiate was Mr Prickett's prying housekeeper, Miss Scrymgeour. Something really impressive would have to be arranged for her, to account for Cyril's regular visits to the flat − after all, not one of the composer's musical friends, obviously not one of his increasingly upper-class acquaintance. Just a good-looking, lower-class boy to her.

Not for nothing was Mr Prickett a devious character, who loved elaboration. After all, was he not becoming known as a genius at scoring? His later friend thought him no such dab at melody; he could never remember a single tune from Johnnie's music, as he could from Elgar's. He was an Elgarian.

At that time, Elgar being still alive, it was fashionable among the younger people up-and-coming to decry Elgar − as they did Kipling. They considered him vulgar.

'I hate his guts,' said Johnny one day.

'Wait until you have written anything half so good before you say that,' said his friend — who was never quite forgiven for his candour.

However, the scheme Prickett thought up was well worthy of the Master for its indirection and elaboration.

He was to 'lose' a wad of musical notes, in an envelope addressed to himself, at the corner of the street where they had turned in that first memorable evening. The envelope would be dropped by Mr Prickett on his way out, just in time for Cyril to pick it up and bring it to Miss Scrymgeour.

She was suitably impressed. 'You must come back when Mr Prickett is at home for him to thank you personally.'

She was not averse to the idea of squeezing a pound out of her tenant, so careful of his money. She knew a thing or two.

Mr Prickett was even more impressed when handed the package containing his notes. 'Invaluable! You have no idea, Miss Scrymgeour, how important they are to me. I don't know if you realise how it is — but when a theme comes into your head, you have to note it down *at once* before it goes out of your head, or gets overlaid by something else. Once you have lost it, it is like looking for a needle in a haystack. And I had the notes for a whole act of an opera in that envelope. Think of it!'

Miss Scrymgeour was grateful for this insight into the creative process from the Master, never one to throw away many confidences about his affairs.

'I am more grateful to the young fellow than I can say. We must get his address and ask him to tea.'

'He looked a very respectable youth,' said Miss Scrymgeour approvingly.

And so he was. It proved the first of many such teas. And not only teas, but visits to the cottage in the country, week-ends and holidays, swimming and gardening. There grew up a firm friendship between Cyril and Johnny, good for both of them.

*

Then came the war. Johnny and Cyril kept sketchily in touch — though Mr Prickett, becoming more and more famous, found more and more young friends. He gained an additional public as composer for the Young.

Cyril had a fine war-record. He was taken prisoner, but made his escape. He got some war-medal or other for his exploit.

When it was all over he came to see his old friend. There turned up a splendid specimen of a man: now broad-shouldered and well filled out, sun-tanned, lines of the face hardened, but the same winning smile.

After a few months back in 'Civvy Street', Cyril confided his dissatisfaction with post-war Britain. He saw no prospect for himself and didn't fancy what he did see. He had an idea that he would do better in a new young country.

Johnny was going to New York for the first production of a new opera, and took Cyril along with him.

By this time a great many doors were open to Johnny in New York and he had a wide circle of acquaintance. One of these was the wife of a business head of one of the vast pharmaceutical concerns that make such fortunes out of American valetudinarianism, their interest in their aches and pains.

This lady, interested in the arts, was a devotee of Prickett's operas. Johnny told her all — or not precisely all — about his *protégé*.

With typical enthusiasm she asked the young officer along to a dance she was giving for young people, for some cause or other. And what should happen there but that her daughter, heiress to millions, fell head over heels for the young fellow — splendid looks and bearing, the romantic allure of escape from prison-camp, and the bonus Britishers enjoyed at that time from the popularity of Winston Churchill, gallant little Britain, etc. (Since then, we have had to 'work our passage' indeed.)

But, of course, the affair could not be encouraged — not a suitable match for a Pharmaceutical heiress.

What was she to do?

She put the problem to Prickett, ever ready with an answer to everything.

He proposed that Cyril should be given a posting in the firm, but far off in California. If he turned out well, after a fair trial — and Cyril believed he would — he could be sent abroad, given a job elsewhere, anywhere in the world, since the firm was world-wide.

*

And so it came about. Cyril passed through his apprenticeship in the firm with flying colours, and was given a posting abroad in Australia.

A good contacts-man, as we have seen, he proved a first-class business executive. In a matter of a few years he was head of the firm in Sydney, well married to the daughter of an old colonial fortune in New South Wales, who would have considered herself more than an equal for any American pharmaceutical heiress.

Rich and prosperous, with a family of a couple of sons, whenever Cyril comes to London on business he has a suite at Claridge's and is well able to entertain Johnny — 'Uncle Johnny' to the boys — on business expenses.

Johnny, almost as well off as he is famous, is well able to put up at Claridge's at his own expense. But he has always been a careful sort, and is content to accept the hospitality of his successful *protégé* on his visits now to old London.

Johnny is vastly amused too — he has a queer sense of humour that appears now and again in his operas — and looks back over the story with evident satisfaction. He teases Cyril sometimes with what would have happened if he had made such a success of it in England: he would inevitably have been knighted. He could have taken for his coat-of-arms a Red Bicycle — no one has thought of that, not even Lord Nuffield, who manufactured it. And for motto, he could take Shakespeare's: *Non sans droict*.

XVII

The Lunatic of Landegey

How to describe the beauty of the inner Fal country, with its chaplet of lovely names, not all of which can I interpret? Tregothnan at the heart of it, I suppose it to be the old homestead in the valley; Mellingoose is straightforward — the mill in the wood; Nancarrow, the valley of the deer; Lamorran, the holy place (Lan means a sacred enclosure, of a saint or such) by the sea; Ardevora veor, the great water; Penkevil, head or tail of the horse's ground.

And what of the names of the parishes, the dedications of the ancient churches to the Celtic saints? Ruan Lanihorne, of St Ruan; St Michael Penkevil, Philleigh and Feock; St Clement, St Allen, St Just-in-Roseland?

What about Old Kea, or Landegey — the lan or sacred spot, of what? Such was its name centuries before Domesday.

Though within a dozen miles of my native home — 'as the crow flies,' the Cornish say — I had never penetrated to that magical, sequestered spot. 'But I am not a crow, and I don't fly,' said downright old Bishop Temple when lost in these lanes, on his way to service and inquiring his way of a rustic. We Cornish are devious and can't possibly explain how to get to anywhere in straightforward manner, and the Bishop was notoriously impatient.

In any case, what an intricate network of lanes, many of them leading to a dead end at river or head of a creek, down a deep combe to tidal beach or quiet reach, the woods coming down to the water's edge!

Such a place was Landegey, or Old Kea. Though I had

never got as far down those lanes, I knew that there was the ruined tower of the old church above the waterside at the very end — and thence no further.

We turned off the main road from Truro at Playing Place — where the medieval miracle plays were performed, I take it: in Cornish, a *plan-an-gwary*. Past the road to Calenick, at the bottom that exquisite Queen Anne house, slate-hung and with pretty cupola over stables — the snuggest place in winter (and the stuffiest in a hot summer).

Then past Carlyon, the farm whence that sad family takes its name — the name Tristram appearing in it regularly over the centuries. On past the turnings that lead to shadowy King Harry Ferry among the dark woods and Trelissick of the beautiful garden; through the little village of Porth Kea, beyond which I had never explored.

At the gate to Lamb Creek farm we stopped to get our bearings and look over the countryside.

How to describe it from this gentle eminence, this plateau of a field, large and flat for Cornwall?

The whole country, on a September day, looked like a green mantle, rippling in folds, here lighter pasture, there a darker streak of woodland — through a breach in a nut-hedge a reach of river, with the grey cottages of Malpas looking down on the water. Malpas — Maupas of the French romances: where Tristram crossed the river, to find Iseult waiting for him, lying on a bank on the other side of the ferry.

And there — a tiny prick into the feathery furrowed sky, a few floating wisps of white cloud — what must be the vane on the central spire of the cathedral at Truro. Only four miles away, and we were in lost, enchanted country.

Already now we glimpsed the ruined tower, two or three of its pinnacles standing, the Gothic tracery of windows shivered, as in some eighteenth-century Gothic folly. And that, indeed, is how it came to be preserved, when the old church fell into ruin — no inhabitants here — and a new church was

156

built across the road into Truro, for the benefit of the miners (who went to chapel with Billy Bray anyway).

How came the church to be in this remote spot, right at the end of the parish, on this tongue of land, where there never can have been many inhabitants?

Easy to see — for here was the tiny head of the creek, where the Saint would have landed from his boat. In those early days, the Age of the Saints, travelling by water was so much easier than by land. It is well known that numerous saints crossed from Wales to Cornwall and on to Brittany in those days, sailing on millstones. My friend, an eminent archaeologist, has his explanation. The coracles, in which the Celts went by water, were (like themselves) very volatile: they needed something to balance them. What better than a small millstone, the hole at the centre convenient for fixing a pole — for mast — up with your sail, and away over those western waters!

So the Saint landed on this spot, thereafter held sacred. Up to the last century a great stone trough was preserved, as the vessel in which he had arrived — looking very much like a petrified coracle. For my part, a modern sceptic, I believe nothing of the kind. I think that this was the fountain into which the water from the neighbouring spring trickled. Beside a spring, or holy well, in Cornwall the saint usually settled, performed his ablutions (if at all), drank his fill with his crust of bread and his honeycomb, and baptised us heathen.

What is historically certain is that this sequestered spot thence had priority over Kenwyn, the much more populous end of the parish — today a large suburb of Truro. It was but a dependent chapelry of Old Kea, and I suppose that that fact is revealed — to the perspicacious eye, in its very name. That just shows you.

*

But the ruined church tower of Old Kea, or Landegey, has another, more recent memory — as recent as the eighteenth century, and that is quite recent here in the Land of the Saints. All but yesterday, you might say.

Is it a memory, or a ghost, that haunts the tower? Here only folklore, the living tradition, can help us.

The memory is that, in Georgian times, a man was shut up in the roomy bottom stage of the tower: no lunatic asylums, or mental hospitals, in those days. This was a convenient sequestered spot — church already removed, upper stages of the tower emptied of bells, going to ruin, the lowest roofed, with slits for windows, a strong oak door barred; the place more or less watertight, but not wind-free. Or was it he who sometimes howled on moonlit winter nights? For he was a moonstruck lunatic.

Who was he?

*

His story is not invented by me. The historian is incapable of such a thing. It is based on facts, and here are the facts, so far as I have been able to elicit them.

The poor fellow who spent his last years boxed up there was a labourer on the neighbouring estate, who laboured under the delusion that he had found a crock of gold under a stone there.

Nothing harmful in that, is there? People have laboured under worse delusions than that — and lived out their lives without harm to anyone.

And old Michael Dungey was harmless enough to everyone in the parish — except to one man, against whom he had an obsession and whose life he threatened. But that man was the Squire of the manor, his former employer. And in those days, in so remote, unfrequented a spot the Squire's word — he was Justice of the Peace and of the Quorum too — was law.

His life had been threatened — was under threat so long as old Michael was free and on the loose: better to shut him up and take no chances.

But what had happened between the Squire and his man to bring about such a state of affairs?

The parish, which knows everything, knew the true story, but was wise enough to keep quiet — since the Squire was their Squire too, owned all the land thereabouts and just about their very souls.

Local folklore preserved the core of the matter in its tradition, and turns out to have been not far wrong. Old Michael *had* found, if not a crock of gold under a stone, leastways an old oak box crammed with gold coins. And he had been wronged.

*

The Squire, in putting Michael under duress and restraint, had provided a regular pittance for his keep. For the rest, the few farming folk of that end of the parish kept him in the luxuries he savoured most — tobacco and snuff, an occasional noggin of brandy: both landed conveniently enough — nothing said to the excise-men, who winked an eye and took what Providence brought to them — up the creek with the incoming tide.

Few were those who had seen the old man — but once seen, never forgotten. Dark and sallow by nature, no need to wash, his skin was of the texture and hardness of leather. He could squash bee or wasp in his hands like horn — no fear of sting penetrating. And his smell! — the natural smell of man in his wild state, but compounded with brandy, and snuff, and the tobacco that came in from the American plantations in those days, in shiny black coils like a snake. They called it 'twist'. Michael rolled it lovingly in those horny hands, but did not smoke: he chewed it.

It had not always been with him like that, though he had never married when young, was something of a solitary and given to dreams.

One night he had a dream that came to him with the force of a revelation — that if he dug under a stone, much overgrown,

159

at the cross-roads he would find gold. He was to dig by the light of the moon, not by daylight, nor at full moon, but at the waning of the moon, when the moon itself was but a wafery crescent of gold in the sky.

He duly awaited the harvest moon's decline from its glory, lighting up all that landscape, ripple and gleam upon creek and river and gold of stubble. With only a glimmer, at dead hour of night, no one about — he could hear the foxes barking, owls hooting in the woods — he worked and dug and levered away at that stone.

It was, in historical fact, no ordinary stone. A large flat surface, it was a shaped stone: the base of an ancient cross that had stood there in the Middle Ages, and perhaps long before — where, in the ages of faith, the infrequent passer-by knelt to say a prayer, or a solitary traveller recognized gratefully the way to the creek. The Reformation, and the centuries that followed, swept scores, if not hundreds, of such objects of devotion all over Cornwall into oblivion, or turned them into gateposts.

At last the dream was fulfilled. Michael hit upon his box, found it full of coins, and replaced the stone.

*

The Squire, passing by one day, noticed the interference. Not for nothing was he a Scawen, a weasely, rational kind of man, given to natural philosophy and mechanical science (he had been at Cambridge): a pure Whig. He didn't hold with folklore and traditions, history and old superstitions. He one day said of the Earl of Clarendon's great *History of the Rebellion*, recently issued from the University Press at Oxford, that for *his* part he was prepared to let bygones be bygones.

A practical attitude that suited the interests of his family very well.

My friend the Cornish historian used to say that he had the impression that these Scawens, who had come into this delectable paradise as recently as only the reign of Queen Elizabeth, had ruffled and scuffled and cuckooed everybody else out of the nest — beginning with the Penkevils. But these had made the mistake of remaining Catholic when the country went Protestant, and got themselves squeezed out as Recusants, paying heavy fines for the luxury of not attending church.

The Scawens made no such mistake: they were always to be found on the winning side or — even more prescient of them — the side that was going to win. At the time of the Civil War, since Parliament was inevitably going to win, they were Parliamentarians. When the King came back at the Restoration they were good monarchists. But, when the Stuarts were sent packing with the Glorious Revolution, the Scawens were glorified as Whigs. And so, when the Hanoverians came in, with German George I — an event not long before that of our story — the Scawens were in clover.

History shows us, my friend would conclude, that it is not the meek who inherit the earth, but the sleek. (The Cornish pronounce this word 'slick'.)

*

The Squire was a slick customer: it did not take him long to get out of his old retainer what he had found. A word had gone round the creek as to a certain gold coin Dungey had exchanged for an unwontedly large consignment of 'run' brandy and tobacco. Poor Michael's addiction to these articles betrayed him — though later a consolation in distress.

The Squire, of course, claimed the gold as his right — found on his land, he said. Michael Dungey knew nothing of the rights and wrongs of treasure-trove, but he did know that the find had been made not on the Squire's land but on the highway at the cross-roads.

But could he take his case to a court of law? Not on your

life. In all this neighbourhood the Squire was the law, and the Medes and the Persians too. And if, *per impossibile*, a case came up to Assizes — in those days at Launceston — his was the most powerful voice in those days of the Whig ascendancy.

He got the gold. It came in very handy to buy a parcel of land nearby to round off his estate at that point — the irregularity of the boundary had irked his mathematical mind as if it were an intrusion.

What old Michael got, with the obsessive mind of the Cornish, was a fixation that he had been wronged. And, also like a Celt, he was bent on revenge. He once and again menaced the Squire, until he thought it safest to shut him up.

Yet Michael had his revenge. From within his confinement in the tower, from that spot sacred to the Saint, he put a curse upon the land acquired with *his* gold. No oxen, cattle or sheep could be kept on that land, it was found — unless marked with a cross, and not only a cross but cross-keys. The Saint himself was in it.

It was this authentic tradition, carried down for generations in the parish lore, that led me to the inwardness of Michael Dungey's story.

XVIII

The Dream House

The Visiting Professor from England was struck by it the moment he saw it. Every day as he passed his eyes were attracted by the shapely lines, the elegance of the little house, which he saw had been specially 'architected', the child of someone's fancy. He described it to his friends as 'both distinguished and sweet'. They came to know that he had a fixation upon it.

They thought it rather odd of him — but it was nothing like so strange as the story of it: the strangest in the world, he thought, before the days of people changing their sex — a theme to which it bore some analogy.

The house stood back on its own in a street of conventional red-brick houses on the slopes of the little university town in eastern Tennessee, a levelled out mountain above overlooking the scene of a battle in the Civil War, otherwise the War between the States.

The house of the Professor's dream was little more than a square box, but it had a front door of distinction of design and woodwork, similarly with the one window beside it, the corners of the walls ribbed with shallow blocks of bricks to punctuate them. But the brickwork, unlike the other houses, was cream-washed, the woodwork painted a pale malachite. Someone of taste had lived there.

For the house was now empty, had been empty for some time. This added to its attraction in the eyes of the romantically inclined stranger to those parts. The unswept winter leaves piled up on the lawn, the débris of fallen sticks, the mess of litter in one corner with an attractive woman's cotton scarf, all muddied and creased, which nobody had bothered to salvage.

He picked his way across the unkempt grass to look in at the window. A wisp of sunlight came in from the back across the polished floor, the whole ground floor one L-shaped room with a fine large Georgian fireplace; in the cove, partitioned off, would be kitchen and scullery.

He sidled round, peering in. A wan light lit up the interior, basement in some disrepair, litter on a spacious back porch, a rambler rose overgrown, unpruned; the back garden curtained off by the draperies of evergreens. Complete, unwonted privacy – unlike other premises open, in the American manner, to every eye, nothing secret, nothing to hide.

The Professor came to identify himself with this beautiful, deserted house, with its air of forlornness. He never passed without eyeing it inquiringly; nobody told him anything about it, who owned it, or why it was deserted in that street peopled by families, children, students, dogs, all the boredom of ordinary domestic life. There was evidently some mystery about it.

As the spring came on, and nobody ever entered or left, a great dogwood came out, overarching the house with its pink glory, as if protecting it, sequestering the whole place, claiming it.

But *who* had lived there, leaving evidences of having loved it?

As he went up to the door one evening there came into his mind the words of a favourite poet:

> 'Is there anybody there?' said the Traveller,
>   Knocking on the moonlit door . . .
> 'Tell them I came, and no one answered,
>   That I kept my word', he said.

164

Then, one grey evening before he left the vicinity — sad at leaving the community where he had been welcome and was happy, sadly reflecting that he would never see the house of his dream again — he was vouchsafed a vision.

There appeared at an upper window, at the side looking down the street, a face. It was a very strange face, for it was mahogany-coloured; a last shaft of light from the west showed that it was that of a white woman, not a black, sharp features, fair hair going grey, dishevelled all about her ears. She had a distraught look, yet intense, as if searching for someone down the sunset street.

A fading glimpse, and it was gone, only a wan shimmer upon the pane.

Had he really seen anything? Or was it hallucination? Actually he was not given to 'seeing things', and did not believe in ghosts.

But perhaps, rationally, this was indeed the association of the house, accounted for its mystery, its desertedness and why nobody would take it on in that family street. And mayn't it have been that he was on its wave-length, himself in some unaccountable way associated with the story?

There are odd coincidences in life that cannot be accounted for. At home in England he had had recounted to him the rarest story that he had ever heard of, either in literature or in his experience.

He had become acquainted with a tall upstanding American veteran, who had fought in the D-day operations across the English Channel. The American invasion forces had been based in the West Country, all along the coast, and here had been the springboard for Dan's brave descent, with his company from his landing-craft, upon Normandy that unforgettable 6th of June.

He had married, but by the time he came back to England as a graduate student after the war, he was a widower – young to have lost his wife, and inconsolable.

Their relations had been, to the conventional mind of his English acquaintance, well-nigh incredible. It was not only that the nature of this big upstanding fellow was essentially feminine – that was within the range of the Professor's experience. And, to console the inconsolable, mitigate the loneliness and despair, he had a familiar, indeed obvious remedy.

'Why not a homosexual relationship? Have you thought of that?'

'Yes. I have considered it.'

'Well, why not? What's wrong with that?'

'I've thought of trying it. But it wouldn't do.'

'Why ever not?'

The Professor was some years older, not many, than the handsome young veteran, who had had a good fighting record, and he pondered. For a few moments he considered the possibilities of the situation, played with them in his mind as if in inverted commas, but made no offer.

Not that it would have been welcomed – he was not sure of that, but in any case was not going to commit himself.

It was just as well – that possibility was closed by the next move that came from the younger fellow:

'It just wouldn't meet the case.'

Whatever was the case then? Just what was the matter with this serious-minded fellow with the haunted expression, as if he had an obsession?

The obsession was revealed, to the older man's astonishment, for he had never heard the like. But, though astonished, he at once understood, for he too was an obsessive type.

The fact was, all too improbably, that the younger man,

completely masculine physically, a big, heavily made fellow, was really a woman by nature.

The professor took a quick look at the large frame, and noticed for the first time a suspicious slope of the shoulders, a certain softness of line.

But a further surprise was in store for him: the young veteran was not only a woman, but his nature was Lesbian. That was why a relationship with a man would not 'meet the case': a normal enough variation in the whole gamut of sex. What he needed was, not a common-or-garden heterosexual relationship with a woman — one could hardly say the opposite sex — but a relationship with another Lesbian who would accept him for one.

This unique relationship he had achieved — against a million chances — and briefly enjoyed. And lost.

Here was the tragedy — and the inconsolability — for it could never be retrieved. At least, in this life.

But might there not be another?

He had come to think so.

For, before his wife died, they had come to share religious belief too.

They had been happy together, and grateful for happiness; for it was less than one chance in a million that they should ever have found each other.

His wife, though made on a smaller scale, was very much like him, fair and blue-eyed. They might have been taken for brother and sister.

They were utterly devoted, and of one mind; shared the same interests, read the same books, indeed read them together. They loved out-door life, and went about the country camping together.

To simplify matters he had tried making over his appearance, growing his hair long like a woman. But that didn't work: he was too tall and heavily made.

They were so happy in each other, and in their unique discovery — when neither could have hoped ever to happen on another like-minded with themselves, who could fit the pattern — that they decided that, if one were to be afflicted with an incurable disease, such as cancer, they would die together.

A suicide pact — they even decided on the way they would go out: in their boat on their lake in the country. They would bore a hole in the bottom and sink with it.

When they were converted to religious belief, such a resolve had to be excluded.

Giving up the idea of living as another woman, Dan resumed his masculine appearance and got a job in the university in the foothills of the Appalachians in Tennessee. There the pair were accepted as a normal couple, happily married man-and-wife, and set up house in a modest way, no one penetrating the secret of their relationship.

Their idyllic happiness in the little home to which they became attached was brief enough, for Dan's wife did develop an incurable disease.

Was it leukemia? Some condition of the blood that turned her to the colour of mahogany.

Both were distraught. No easy way out now, by suicide pact: their religious belief forbade it.

Accidentally, Dan's end came first. Always a rather haphazard driver, his mind on other things, careering about in a rickety old motor car, he was driving riskily down that steep western street on ice, when his brake failed and he crashed into the ravine at the bottom.

His wife lived not long after the accident. Was that her face the Professor glimpsed at the upper window, searching down the westering street at sunset for Dan?

For theirs was the community to which Dan's former

acquaintance had by chance been invited, and coincidentally theirs had been the haunting little house which so strangely obsessed him on his visit.

XIX

The Wax Doll

It was maddening that it should be this particular house that was burned down, for it was, strictly speaking, about the most perfect architecturally in the West Country.

West Country houses are rarely of a perfection. They are often interesting, sometimes beautiful; but they are frequently irregular, built at different periods, added on to — today, in our time of decline, more frequently subtracted from.

But Tremans remained intact right up to the 1930's, when everything went wrong.

The curious thing was that no one ever discovered who its architect was. It was entirely in the style of Gibbs, regular tall windows, diminishing in height with each storey, every one with a subtle, hardly decipherable inward inclination towards the top. Front door with a shell porch over, three granite steps up to it. Regularity; symmetry; elegance.

Within, even more so: a grand wooden staircase, richly turned balusters going up from the front hall; most of the rooms panelled in painted pine panelling — Queen Anne. It would burn like matchwood, somebody said; and it did. There was no saving it, it burned so quickly — only a few objects of not much value were got out; among them one, a curiosity one would not have expected to survive.

The place had just been done up to the nines, the restoration nearly complete, when a workman left a blow-lamp burning, against a shutter up in an attic. Before anyone was aware — the family away — the whole place was ablaze.

Was it carelessness? Or deliberate sabotage?

Two positions were taken on the matter locally. A West Countryman of more than local reputation, something of an aesthete, enraged by the irreparable loss, was convinced that it was sabotage. Carelessness was hardly less culpable. What did the fool of a workman care about the loss of something rare and irreplaceable?

The aesthete — with the ruthlessness of his kind — favoured punishment befitting the crime. A Philistine architect let loose on Oxford was known for his addiction to 'punched face', i.e. a rough dressing of stone which collected smears of grime and dirt all over the building. The West Countryman thought that it should be applied to the architect, rather than the building.

Similarly with the perpetrator of the crime at Tremans. How would that workman like the application of the blow-lamp to himself? A work of art was unique and could never be replaced; a type like him was all too easily replaceable.

Moreover, the man who reflected thus knew the odd story of the house, which made it all the more affecting to him.

*

The family itself was something out of the common for the West Country, for they were of Huguenot stock that had come in through business under William and Mary. Their concerns brought them to Exeter at its most flourishing — then the sixth city in the realm. Perhaps they brought the plan of their house ready-made from London, and the excellent West Country builders and craftsmen carried it out. Exeter had its own school of decorative plasterers, who worked all over the West Country. 'Italian artists', said the Victorians, who had lost the tradition — along with the sense of proportion that went with it.

By Victorian days the vital impulse of the family had given

out; they had become more than usually dull country gentry — really not up to the house they had inherited, unappreciative of its beauty. They filled it with the usual Victorian encumbrance of bamboo furniture, palms, ferns, bric-à-brac, knick-knacks, *bibelots*, Aunt Louisa's tatting. As often happens, it was only at the end that they came to realise its distinction, and set about clearing out the rubbish that had accumulated.

One object, however, they did not touch, it was so bound up with the family story.

In those Victorian days, when the event was frequent enough, and yet — though covered up and made into a great secret, which everybody knew — a daughter of the house had had an illegitimate baby. A blot on the scutcheon — as Browning wrote.

What more natural, when the poor young lady, not very bright in the head, had no marriage in prospect and was confronted by — exposed to, one might say — a handsome, sexy young footman day by day, night by night?

'I only wish it was me,' said a candid kinswoman of the family — but she was safely beyond the age of parturition, her rather cynical candour not approved by those closer to the event.

The footman was, of course, dismissed; the poor young lady sent off on an Italian tour for the benefit of her health — really to one of those establishments in Maida Vale, where young ladies of good family retired to have their unwanted babies.

The young lady's was far from unwanted — by her. It was the only object in life she cared for — fruit of the only experience of life that had come her way, her all too brief happiness.

But, of course, it could not be accepted, recognised, by the family.

When she returned from her Italian tour the baby was put

out to nurse at an establishment at Torquay, which became notorious. For at just that time it created a great scandal.

Charlotte Winsor's was only one of many such places, where infants were taken in for a lump sum down, and then left to die. Starvation? Laudanum − that favourite Victorian sedative − in their gruel? It was difficult to bring home responsibility, infant mortality was so high − from scarlet fever, measles, smallpox, diphtheria, typhoid, bad drains.

Charlotte Winsor's case was exposed, however; tried for murder, she escaped hanging only by a legal technicality.

The young lady of Tremans could not but hear of the case, and hers was one of the infants that had thus disappeared.

This completed her disarray: she became 'low on her mind', as we say in the West Country. Not exactly demented, she lapsed back into childhood, with an absolute obsession about her child.

Someone had the idea of a substitute − had had a large wax doll made, a fine object, as large as a baby. It worked. The poor creature lived for her 'baby', kept upstairs in her bedroom: she slept with it at night − not encouraged to be seen about with it when there was company.

However, the servants knew. It added another element to the secret that everybody knew.

The poor creature was not long for this world. When she died, the doll was relegated to the corner cupboard in her bedroom, and there safely locked in.

*

But everyone knew of its existence.

And there were curious consequences. Irregular, infrequent, *in*consequent as they seemed, they were not without a pattern.

Men guests who slept in that room never heard a sound. It was only women who − very occasionally − were awakened

173

by what seemed a baby crying. And of the women only a chosen few heard.

It became clear that it was invariably women of the family, or kinsfolk, who heard. And of those, only the unmarried, the childless.

For example, one rather remote cousin from Cornwall, whom one would never expect to hear anything, she was so large and insensitive — looked like a Grenadier Guardsman. She was, not unexpectedly, an old maid; if not precisely old, at any rate a spinster, a frustrated life.

She insisted at breakfast that she had heard an eldritch cry, more like a fatal scream. The old squire told her that what she had heard was the mating cry of a badger. She was unpersuaded.

*

As time passed, less and less was heard from that room — as if that impulse, or relic, of vitality was wearing out too.

A subsequent generation, which had grown up with the story, took it for granted and treated the whole thing lightly. The last head of the family to inhabit the house would occasionally take a curious guest along to the room, unlock the corner cupboard and take out the doll. It was a very fine specimen of Victorian doll-making, just like a small child.

The curious thing was that, though made of wax, it was almost the only thing to come through the fire.

How it had done so was the mystery.

XX

A Holiday by the Sea

He was a mining magnate. And since, in late Victorian days, tin mining was still carried on in some areas of Cornwall, he was a tin-mining magnate. He had that nose for tin characteristic of Cornish folk, that sixth sense which they have carried all round the world. As the old saying goes, 'Wherever there is a hole in the earth, you will find a Cornishman at the bottom of it.' Actually, M.P. — he was always known somewhat pompously, and pomposity was his *faible* — had carried his expertise no further than the London Stock Exchange.

For, well before the fatal year 1914, the mines in his part of East Cornwall had closed down. The high plateau of St Ann's Chapel was his native heath — all that ridge of land from which you can see the Hamoaze estuary running out at Plymouth and Saltash Bridge erected not many decades before.

As for his nose, it was a prominent, exploratory, sexy proboscis, with a tendency to twitch, especially at sight of a nubile girl, when he had a way of running a long forefinger along that slightly dampening organ.

In earlier days he had been a great dab at local preaching in the chapels of the district — Caradon, Harrowbarrow, Calstock, Gunnislake, down that precipitious hill to the Tamar frontier that divides Cornwall from England.

He was, as the Methodists called it, 'on the plan'. In those days there was no good feeling between Church and Chapel, and Anglicans in the district — there were a few — would

175

scoff at his habit of sending round a Christmas message in the following form. First, a few words from 'the Master'; then a few more, from John Wesley; last, *pour comble de tout*, to clinch the matter, some profound thought from M.P. himself.

Whether this was so or no, true it was that he made a regular thing of taking the Bible classes at Sunday Schools with the senior girls, whose breasts were beginning to show ('breast-heavers' the unkind, but observant local historian called them, who kept an eye on the prominent M.P.'s ways).

He was very strong in the pulpit on morality — by which the Cornish always mean sex. It added a spice to his sermons: Hellfire for departing from the strait and narrow path.

All which did not prevent him from suggesting to one of the girls that they should take a walk one evening in the woods.

'Do you think I'd be such a fool?' said she.

For, in fact, he was already a married man, but with a wife not strong, always ailing, not up to him, not enough for him. No children.

*

Now, years later, he was a widower. And had moved to London, to look after his City interests, which were considerable and booming. As Cornish tin went down, Malaysian tin went up. He was handsomely invested in Kuala-Lumpur Consolidated, Koh-i-Nor United, Penang Rubber and Tin Associated, Malaysian this and that.

Balding now — no indication of a lack of sexual potency, rather the reverse, fortified by a large walrus moustache — he had a curious expression in his heavy-lidded grey eyes. An expression at once kindly and sly, sleepy and yet alert: his eyes would light up at a main chance, in several senses.

Not ungenerous — provided he got the credit for what he did in the way of charitable deeds — he was a good deal of a sentimentalist. With an enlarged heart, he could not bear it to be empty.

Nor need it be, for, though eldering, had he not become a magnate in his own right?

*

In the impersonal world of London — such a contrast with the all too personal world of St Ann's Chapel and Caradon — he was 'taking an interest', as we used to say, in a promising widow outside the world of his mining interests.

He needed relief. This she provided.

She had an engaging personality, with rather literary pretensions — she had been secretary to a well-known writer. This appealed to his own pretensions, and a marked element in his make-up: masculine vanity.

No chicken, she looked much younger than her years, from her way of doing her hair in youthful ringlets, carefully arranged around pretty face. Her little snub-nose — always with a dab of powder to conceal any tendency to purple (he was of course a teetotaller, strong on Temperance) — he found adorable. Tip-tilted as it was, it gave an impression of a superior person, as indeed she was.

Her voice, which was not strong, had a way of fading out occasionally: a trait which he found endearing. Sometimes it gave out altogether — and that, appealing to male strength, completed his conquest.

A widow, with a little girl of six or so, she had something in the way of independent means, which — with a pension, for her husband had died in the Boer War — enabled her to keep a nanny. All the same, though a good many years older, her *inamorato* would be a good catch. He had no children, and was fond of her Mavis.

*

On vacation — infrequent enough, for he was an attentive business man, who did not take an eye off his concerns — they occasionally rolled into the country in his large, early

Rolls-Royce. The little girl found it rather seasick-making; however, she had Nanny to attend to her.

For one of their summer holidays he decided on Cornwall — not his own Tamarside, but a neat hide-out of a private hotel on the south coast of mid-Cornwall. In those paradisal pre-1914 days the district had not been popularised, was as yet little frequented, except by the elect.

Gwendreath — the Cornish for white sands — had a beach almost a mile long, of hard shingle not for bathing. At the far end were convenient caves and rock pools. Above the cliffs, pinewoods which scented the air round about.

He had always been partial to a walk in the woods, with a companionable female. And the merry widow was certainly good company, agreeable and willing.

The small party would be seen issuing forth from the hotel, widower and widow together in front, followed at a distance by Mavis and Nanny.

When out of sight he would take his companion's arm — it made a pretty picture, her ringlets lifted by the breeze which brought colour to her face. The little girl was contented enough, tripping down the woodland paths, Nanny in attendance, catching up a little breathless. Nothing much to be said of her — except what was said of a famous Cornishman, Sidney Godolphin, by King Charles II:

'Never in the way, and never out of the way.'

In those days before 1914 signalised the end of civilisation, she knew her place and to keep her mouth shut. Nothing much about her diminutive, youthful appearance either, demure but sufficiently nubile.

A happy family party they looked, with further promise of happiness to come.

Some days they would make their way down the old cliff road to the vast beach, which would engulf them from view by the time they reached the farther end.

Even so, the couple would make themselves comfortable

and at home in one of the caves they came to look on as their own.

Some distance off Mavis and Nanny had plenty to occupy them for hours with sand castles and rock pools, pressing out sea-water from the mamillary sea-anemones, pursuing the tiny scuttling crabs left behind by the retreating tide.

The occupants of the cave also seemed to find plenty to occupy them, out of sight of a morning, until their trek back for lunch — for which the stimulating sea-air redoubled their appetite.

*

Such good times must have an end. Business was calling him back to London.

They would return separately, for the widow was engaged to complete her holiday with a visit to her relations in the West Country, further 'up the line', as we used to say — and indeed her little party was to go up by train. The understanding was that they would meet in London early in the autumn.

All was arranged, in business-like fashion, bills paid, cab to the railway station fixed for next morning — when it was found that the magnate had left late the night before. Not alone, but with the mousey, but indubitably nubile, Nanny.

XXI

The Wise Old Serpent of King's Wood

Why the 'King's Wood'? No one knew. Yet the reason for the tradition was plain and simple.

Before the Civil War — which was such an appalling experience for Cornwall, with armies marching down the little land, eating up its provender, the losses of lives fighting for the King all the way up to Bristol — the whole of Menacuddle parish had been part of the Duchy manor of Trenance. The Duchy of Cornwall was a Crown possession, held on behalf of the King's eldest son.

After the fatal war the King's possessions were sold to pay for the war — to be resumed again at the Restoration when the King's son came back to his own as Charles II. But for some inexplicable reason unknown to the historian, the manor of Trenance did not come back to the King. Why not? Why was it an exception?

The manor had been bought at the sale of the Duchy possessions by a family of small gentry who were Parliamentarians, and they struck a good bargain below its full value. Why was it not restored to the King with the rest of the Duchy lands in the West?

Did money pass? Was there some hanky-panky with the Duchy Receiver, a kinsman of the local family? No one knew, for they destroyed all their papers — no incriminating evidence.

But the local tradition held firm: it was the *King's* Wood, always was, and still is, filling the beautiful valley and running up the eastern side of it to the goodly house the family later built in the reign of Queen Anne. It was called Pennance, which merely means in the old Cornish language the head of the valley. As the Cornish forgot their language and the meanings of the names, they came to attach the English meaning to that somewhat gloomy house, as if overcast, tainted by some original guilt. Which was, the historian thought, indeed the case.

Another tradition attaching to the place went back much further. Local folklore said that in the depths of that dark wood lived a great snake. No one had ever seen him, for people didn't like to penetrate too far into that piece of overhung, prehistoric forest, like Wistman's Wood on Dartmoor.

There were stones too lying about, some of them still upright, going back to the Stone Age, or at least the Age of Bronze, far beyond that of the Saints, of whom we at least still remembered the names and kept their feast-days.

All kinds of folklore attached to those stones: how a horse would shy and refuse to enter their circle; how once in the year, at midsummer, the upright monoliths would revolve in their pits, while the leaning one made obeisance to the sun.

On the western side of the valley was Mulvra — it means the bald hill — with its cairn like a nipple on the breast of the horizon. It was watched by two pillar-like longstones. They were said to come down once a year at night to drink at the stream which had made the valley.

Modern-minded people hearing these tales of the parish shrugged them off saying it was all very rummy. And perhaps it was — more than they knew.

When we were boys we hadn't the least doubt of the existence of that very old and wise snake in the heart of the King's Wood, though we would never go into the depths of it to see. All the same, nothing sinister was ever told of him, and we were too young to know that the snake was the symbol of wisdom, but also of guilt, of original sin. We did not associate

King's Wood with the story of Adam and Eve, for all that we heard about that in church; nor was it our idea of Paradise.

Our wise old serpent was in fact benevolent − no question of making him propitiatory offerings, as in the torrid zone of Mexico or New Mexico. Though no one saw him, he gave sage advice to those in trouble. Very occasionally someone in distress ventured into the depths of the wood to learn what they wanted to know, and heard his whispered advice. Or said they had heard it − perhaps it was the whispering of the leaves around the entrance to his hollow; or the hissing of the stream where the stones came down to drink. Or perhaps just the fancies they carried back from the strangeness of the place. Having ventured so far they had to have something to show for their courage − they might have been laughed at otherwise. And being laughed at, it is well known, is the greatest humiliation in a primitive community.

*

There is always something in a tradition, some nub, if only one can get at it; some nexus, if only one has the patience, or the knowledge to untie it. And that there was *something* at the bottom of it is witnessed by the curious events that attended the end of the family at Pennance in our time.

The family that had been so wide-awake and on the make at the time of the Civil War was teetering towards its end with an only daughter, the heiress, who could hardly be said to be awake at all. Was she quite right in the head? One wouldn't have said so − though no one quite knew, for the family lived a withdrawn life in the last two generations, and the girl was brought up at home, never went to school, in great innocence and ignorance of life. A lonely existence, kept from any rough contacts, consoled by music, her one talent, and devoted to her mother. This naturally fortified her solitariness and helped to fill the inner dream in which she mostly lived out her days. (Later, we shall see, she added a further, more eerie dimension, to explore.)

She was attractive in her way; and if she was rather *décousue* − didn't altogether add up − still she was the heiress, she would in time succeed to the inheritance. And to her mother's own fortune too, which was not inconsiderable. For her father, the squire, in unquestioned possession of the land hereabouts for generations, had married for money, a shade below him, out of the county, indeed out of any county. The mother was apt to say smugly, and with a touch of vulgarity:

'Constance will never need to count her change.'

Constance was thus a desirable *parti*, and it was desirable to see her safely married to a suitable partner. Care was taken to see that the young man was suitable, and in fact the marriage was one of affection. No cold linking together of estates, such as had built up the family's position in previous generations. None of the somewhat brutal harshness of her great-grandfather, who had left a name in the parish and upon his monument in church, as Justice of the Peace:

Merit he noticed − knavery he scorned,
To humble worth a friend! − to rogues a thorn.

In the hungry 1840s there had been a food-riot, and a mob of tin miners had attacked the two lodges that stood on either side of the entrance to the long drive that led to the house. The old squire had thereupon had both of them demolished:

'No more of that nonsense.'

Constance's upbringing had been excessively protected, and she was encouraged to choose for *fiancé* a young fellow of whom she had been fond when they were children and occasionally had lessons together. Since then they had not seen much of each other − Nicky was away at school and university, and then had gone briefly (and briefless) to the bar. His family were not landed gentry, and he was not averse to taking on an estate: he would know how to manage it, and

the gentle, passive, rather abstracted heiress. No problem for
him.

A small country house was acquired for the young couple
to set up house in, down in the valley just outside the boundary of the estate across from the King's Wood.

All went according to plan, and the couple were installed.

What happened next no one quite knew, for all was hushed
up. But it seems that on her wedding night, or shortly after,
Constance escaped from the embraces of her husband and —
distracted — rushed in her nightdress, a white wraith in the
moonlight, through the King's Wood and up the hillside,
home to Pennance and mother.

The explanation? No one knew. No brutality on the part of
the husband, for Constance later seemed quite fond of him,
though living safely apart. It seems that, never having been
brought up against the facts of life, indeed left uninstructed
in them, she was appalled by the revelation when confronted
by what life is about, face to face.

*

A nervous breakdown followed, as a matter of course. Constance never fully recovered her nerve, if she ever had had
any.

After a few years she managed to keep on an even keel.
Away from Pennance, in a home for a time, she found susten-
ance in spiritualism and the practice of Yoga. It was at any
rate a discipline and kept her on the rails. At times she would
go off into a trance, and there — absent in the body, one
didn't know where her mind was — she listened to the
wisdom, the suggestions, that came to her.

The suggestion came that she should consult the wise old
serpent of King's Wood as to her state, and the cause of it. If
she could confront the cause, perhaps that would bring
about its cure — after all, a piece of wisdom completely in
line with the best modern psychotherapy. Nothing very

different – and, strengthened by a definite recommen-
dation, which came to her like a command, she did not know
whence, she proceeded to follow it. After all, were not the
King's Wood and all that was in it hers, or hers to be? Though
a humble soul spiritually, she was not without family pride.
She knew her place in the world, heiress of the family planted
at Pennance since the Civil War. Was there not the portrait
in the hall – a primitive daub, it is true – of the ancestor
who had come by the estate, she did not know how?

The voice – or whatever she heard – from the hollow
cave in the heart of the Wood told her. We do not know what
it said. It is to be presumed that it said that the King's Wood,
nor the estate either, was not rightfully hers or her family's.
Did it advise that it should be restored to the Crown? How
could that be done? – for that was what came to prey upon
her mind.

Her people were failing. She herself passed more and more
of her time in her self-induced trances. Was it that again, in
another form, she could not confront the fact of life, that the
place she knew, to which she was heir – with its original
guilt, or blemish in the possession, or whatever it was – was
not rightfully hers?

We shall never know, for in one of these trances, seated
cross-legged on the floor like a Buddha, she passed out of this
life, guilt or no guilt.

And still the King's Wood has not been recovered to the
Crown.

XXII

Sailors' Orchard

Not far inland, between the tiny port of Porthtowan and the no less tiny inlet of Polmear, was a delicious little hollow that seemed to hold a secret for the dedicated local recorder. Whenever he passed that secluded spot upon the unfrequented coast road − a lane rather than a road − the place put a spell upon him, stimulated his imagination.

But to what point?

It was as if seeking its story to be told, offering a secret to be penetrated. But what?

Where the road curved round at the bottom of an abrupt declivity, and a stream gushed out at all times of the year from a perennial spring in the field above, was a diminutive orchard.

At last he found out that it had a name: Sailors' Orchard. This provided a clue. Sailors − in those days of little coastal sailing craft, when the bay would be alive at night with a myriad lights of the fishing boats − were in the habit of halting on their way between the two ports to pick apples there, ripe or unripe. And not only to pick apples.

The orchard had come to two sisters, who were the last lives in the lease for three lives, which was very common for copyholders in old days in Cornwall. From the road one could just glimpse the upper two windows, the bedroom windows, of the cottage which went with the orchard − or, rather, the orchard went with it.

No love was lost between the two sisters; the orchard itself provided an apple of discord, over which they could quarrel, though the quarrel proved more serious than that.

The elder of the two, Joanna, was small and rather pretty, fair and blue-eyed, a neat, trim figure; but she was unmarried. The younger, Jemima, large and dark and rather bossy, had got herself a husband by the little harbour of Porthtowan: a big, burly fellow, who earned his living as a carpenter, good tempered and easy-going.

They had no children, however, and Jemima, not easy to live with, became more and more morose; she held on to her Jim, a steady sort of fellow — she had him in her clutches, as she thought.

With the younger sister thus provided for, it seemed only right to Joanna to hold on to the old home and the orchard, though she couldn't live off apples alone.

No means of dividing the little bit of property, as in the neighbouring harbour of Polmear. There two brothers — both as mean as catshit — had divided everything in their parents' house. When it came to the big double-bed, in which they had been born, they simply sawed it in two. Each of them, unmarried, had then a single bed.

We were so poor in those days — a fair number of us couldn't afford to marry; those two brothers, fishermen and beachcombers — with a seagull's eye for what the sea might throw up — wouldn't have married anyhow.

So Joanna was left high and dry in the cottage overlooking the orchard, with just a glimpse of the road; the orchard prettier even than herself, in spring when all white and starry with apple-blossom in which the birds sang; or again in autumn when the fruit was ruddy and gold, in which the birds darted about, pecking away.

She was left poor, but was hard-working, not without spirit and her own leaning to independence, a spark of determination, though without her sister's bossiness. She took in washing — did all the laundry for the big house over the hill. Neat and tidy, she kept her house spotless, as spotless as herself — though perhaps that was not the word for it in all respects.

187

For, of course, orchard and garden plot and all the washing — that was not enough to keep body and soul together. She had to have another line beside the washing-line.

Well, there was the occasional sailor stopping by her orchard below to pick the fruit. What more convenient than to nip off the road, up through the orchard, and into the snug little house, snug between sheets?

It wasn't always convenient for Joanna, of course. It was easy to provide a signal for those who recognised it — for whom it was meant — whether it was or not. When it was not convenient for her to receive a visitor, a duster was fixed in the bedroom window which could be glimpsed from below: in marine idiom, her 'rag was up.' When the coast was clear, and all was well, the bedroom window was open, free as air.

Thus Joanna made ends meet, kept the wolf from the door, or whatever, perhaps called the prowling, provident wolf within door.

Of course, the inevitable happened, and Joanna found herself with child. Nobody knew who the father was, perhaps not even the mother herself. This added further to the difficulty of making a livelihood, providing means of subsistence; when all was so poor in the human landscape, so restricted in outlook or prospect — Joanna hardly ever went further than her pretty legs could carry her, to neighbouring Porthtowan, say.

*

Then, in this not very moral tale, a dramatic turn — might one say for the good? — came about in her circumstances. On one of her visits to Porthtowan, Jim felt her attractions superior to those of her sister; though married to Jemima, he could put up with her no longer.

A simple-minded, good hearted fellow, Jim hardly argued the matter out with himself: he just took off one day and set up in the cottage above the orchard with the altogether more amenable and better-tempered Joanna.

Ructions followed, in the harbour village of Porthtowan, where everybody's business was everybody else's, and a highly moral censoriousness offered peculiar pleasure — an outlet they would have been shocked to be told the origin of.

Tongues clacked like the clapper of a mill; parties formed: though no one declared openly in favour of living in open sin, not many held with the wronged, but unsympathetic, Jemima.

In the simple circumstances of those days, divorce was not to be thought of: an even greater scandal, and there simply was not the money for it. Even if Jemima had been willing to accommodate her sister, which she was not. She did not hold with her sister in any wise: she was the respectable one, the moral one, the situation now openly showed up her sister as a bad woman. She did not even go to chapel, as Jemima did — had never done so since they parted company and Joanna took to her deplorable ways.

Even Joanna, whose nature was kindlier and more receptive than Jemima's, felt some guilt at having stolen her sister's husband — she sometimes blushed when she thought of it, a nice apple pink showing in her fair skin. This did not make her less attractive in the eyes of Jim, and soon custom eroded any feeling of awkwardness, the situation accepted.

The fact was that Joanna and Jim found that they were made for each other. Both of an equable disposition, they were as happy as a couple of birds, as 'happy as the days are long', as we say.

Joanna had the more spiritedness, a little spark to her. And now, confident in her new-found happiness, she made a mistake. It all went to prove that one mustn't tempt good fortune too far, one's luck won't hold. (The local fishermen and sailors all knew that.)

Jim's earnings were pretty small and, as a carpenter, irregular; three in the house, with the baby, they were still hardly above subsistence level. Joanna bethought her of putting in a claim for parish pay for the baby — after all, it was not Jim's, and she herself an unmarried mother. Even five shillings a week, the usual rate, would make all the difference to the little household.

But she reckoned without her sister.

When Joanna's case came before the high and mighty magistrates in the county town — in those days J.P.'s from their country houses unaware of the circumstances in remote and sequestered Sailors' Orchard — her sister Jemima also appeared in court.

When the J.P.'s were inclined to be sympathetic to the trim and respectable-looking little figure Joanna made, her sister 'up and spoke', as the local people reported:

'She've bin and taaken away my man.'

On inquiry from the big-wigs, this could not be denied. No parish pay was forthcoming. Life at Sailors' Orchard continued almost as restricted as before, though the little cottage knew contentment and happiness, and no longer was there any need for tracks from the roadside over the hedge and in under the trees, under spring blossom or autumn fruit.

On the other hand, local folk held that the Orchard was haunted. Though they never *saw* anything, whose were the unaccountable tracks in the morning or evening dew?